Try the Goose Grease

Try the Goose Grease

TALES OF A YOUNG NURSE
IN RURAL PEI DURING THE EARLY
TWENTIETH CENTURY

MARY ISABEL TUPLIN

Registration Number: 1192815
Type: Copyright
Author: Tuplin, Mary Isabel
Owner: Kormos, Lori / Nunes, Fern / Nunes, Joseph
Registration Date: 2022-05-0

ISBN numbers:
978-1-7781772-0-0 (book)
978-1-7781772-1-7 (e-book)
978-1-778772-2-4 (hardcover book)

NOTE: The stories that take place in this novel are from
the first half of the twentieth century and thus the language
reflects that time in history. The words "Indian" and
"Micmac" have not been removed because they were
commonly used at the time the book was written.

Table of Contents

continues

Foreword

This is the third edition of the novel *Try the Goose Grease*! Written and illustrated by my grandmother, Dolly Tuplin (nee Mary Isabel MacDonald), it depicts the career of a nurse in rural PEI in the early part of the twentieth century. Goose grease was a well-known remedy in folk medicine, and caregivers to the sick were often urged to use it for their patients – hence the title. The book was first published by Dolly's daughter, Ann Tuplin Nunes, and editor Patricia Stanyer, owner of Aldergrove Publishing Company.

In rural areas of the province, a nurse would be required to take up residence at the home of a patient and undertake the burden of care with only short visits from a doctor. Without the benefits of the equipment and staffing levels provided in hospital care, a nurse who chose country nursing did so out of love for the landscape and the people who lived a quiet existence, away from the noise and lights of the city. Such was the case with the main character, nurse Elizbeth MacRae, whose experiences were based on Dolly's own nursing career.

In several chapters, Dolly writes about cases of Spanish Influenza. Her stories describe the coughing and danger of pneumonia, the risk to the elderly, the closure of schools and the recommendation to avoid public gatherings and social events, a protocol to be repeated a century later, during the COVID-19 pandemic.

In her description of the novel, Dolly writes, "Almost all the stories were my own experiences, a few were those of other nurses." Upon review of her manuscript, a nurse who trained with Dolly said, "You spoke for all of us."

This edition is dedicated to Dolly and the other nurses of that time, and to my mother, Ann, who spearheaded the compilation and publication of the first edition after Dolly's death in 1975.

Acknowledgement is given to Dolly's nieces, Doris Ewart and Elizabeth (Bessie) Parker, for their efforts towards the publication of the manuscript, and to Georgina Fitzgerald and Mary Parker for their encouragement on the current edition. A special thank you to Liz Bradley who did the graphic design and layout for the novel. Couldn't have done it without you!

To my co-editors on this edition, Fern Nunes and Joe Nunes, thank you for your passion and dedication. I think Granny would be proud!

— Lori Kormos

What Lies Ahead?

Graduation was a time of ostentation and glory. The head nurse, who had trained in England, tied the strings of her cap under her chin. She had also starched her underskirt so that her uniform flared in a grand, impressive way. The graduates wore stiffly starched uniforms with huge puffed sleeves. Our day of glory came when we received our diplomas, pins from Birks, silver-cased thermometers, and flowers. We listened to young Dr. Grant address the graduates. He advised us to "be careful in carrying out the doctors' orders." It smacked of male superiority. He might know we would try to do our best.

Dr. Grant was young but very assertive. Flush from the hallowed halls of McGill medical school, with a gold medal for his academic prowess, he commanded much respect.

We were very much in awe of the doctors! Hospital etiquette had been imparted to each wide-eyed probationer by the head nurse in the ward. "Never speak to the doctors until they speak to you." And if we were seated while making dressings, we were to rise when a doctor entered the room or came from behind a screen. We were admonished by one matron, "If the patient dies, it is your fault."

It was 1917, and although we had trained for three years and could write R.N. after our names, we had no mid-wifery training as they did in some English hospitals. Nor did we have any mental therapy training. But nurses were expected to go where they were asked to go, and no matter how hard the case, they were expected to stay as long as they were needed.

Some nurses were going overseas to work with the Red Cross and in Allied Military Hospitals, but I was not so adventurous. I had registered to do private duty. This meant working in homes on Prince Edward Island for a set rate of five dollars per day if the patient was able to pay for it. There were cases of Spanish Influenza where all in the household were in bed so that the preparing of the meals fell to the nurse, and even some care of the animals in the barn.

My clients hired me from the registry. I rented a room in Brighton, and I went into the country by horse and buggy, or by car if the people could afford the new-fangled monster which was only allowed to run in the afternoons of certain days at that time on Prince Edward Island. Even when I travelled home for a few days in between cases, it was not uncommon for people to come to the door looking for a nurse.

I took comfort from the fields, the trees, the ocean which beat on Island shores, and the turn of the seasons.

Spring, summer, autumn, and winter were realized in the country as they never could be in town. In my brief hours off, I read and sketched. These times were often snatched from my long hours of duty, relieved by a member of the family when the patient was sleeping.

One evening when I was free of a case, I walked from my rooming house to the Prince Edward Island Hospital where I had trained. It was a long way, but there were no buses, and taxis were expensive, so we were used to walking. Because we were usually on our feet for twelve hours or more each day, we often had sore feet, and in time, little bumps and hollows showed through our shoes.

The nurses' home was connected to the hospital and was much travelled day and night. I came to the door of the room I had lately shared with other nurses and was welcomed with screams of joy, "Elizabeth, Elizabeth MacRae!" I was pounced upon and embraced by all. I knew that part of the enthusiastic welcome resulted from the joy of freedom from a twelve-hour duty in the wards and the knowledge that shortly, at nine o'clock sharp, all lights would be out and all would be quiet.

Ann Fisher had been in my class but was not quite through her training because of losing time from illness. She was a tall, willowy girl who had been doing her hair when I came in. It was in short curls on either side of her thin, narrow face with the rest pulled into a bun at the back. She began to complain of how hard it was to please Miss Sharp, the supervisor, and Dr. Grant. If Dr. Grant could only be more like Dr. Burke, we mused, because

Dr. Burke laughed a lot and liked to tell stories – a real Irish wit.

She fastened on me a knowing look. "Now that you're gone, Dr. Grant is not himself. He was always more agreeable when you were on the floors. I wish you would come back," she sighed. I explained, attempting to avoid the intensity of their scrutiny, "It's just that there isn't always work for R.N.'s in the hospital unless people ask for special nurses. I have to take the jobs that are offered. I can't pick and choose as long as I am on the registry," I said regretfully.

Helen Martin, known as just Martin to her friends, came in and began to tell of her experience with the Spanish Influenza. She had been sent out to a house where three young farmers lived, along with an elderly housekeeper: "Two of the men and the housekeeper were very ill with the flu. There was real danger of pneumonia. The third man, Robert, was wonderful at helping me. All night, he kept the fire going in the kitchen wood stove. He slept on a sofa at one side of the kitchen while I occupied the sofa at the opposite end of the long room. We listened for calls from the bedrooms upstairs or for the violent coughing which signalled the need for the cough medicine and chest rubs. Then Robert took the flu. Now I was working alone. But soon the next-door neighbour sent over their hired girl because they knew I had a houseful of sick people. The neighbour also came over to help. He was curious as to who I was and thought he knew my people. He said, 'I knew you were either a Martin or a Camel'. I was pulling a heavy mattress at the time, and I thought from the way he pronounced Campbell that he took me for a beast of burden!"

All laughed at the ludicrous picture described, and then she continued: "They all recovered through time, and as soon as he could travel, Robert hurried off to see his girl! He was engaged. The good ones are always spoken for." She shrugged and we all laughed again.

Martin had trained in the Calgary General Hospital but was home on the Island and was nursing here in the hospital. We had become close friends. She was tall with dark hair and eyes that sparkled with humour and mischief. Quick to see the humorous side of everything, she would sometimes call the two of us, when we walked anywhere together, the "long and short of it."

Good at mimicry, Martin now went into an impersonation of Dr. Grant when he was angry, and one of Miss Sharp, the head nurse. Miss Sharp bent forward at the waist a good deal. She was no longer young, and her bad posture might have been caused by bending over beds in her many years of nursing. But we laughed anyway, and then at Martin's insistence, we all did a chorus line imitation of "Mademoiselle from Armentieres, Parlez-vous?" between the beds in the crowded room. Then the bell rang for lights out, and I left to go back to my room in Brighton. I had missed the camaraderie of the hospital more than I had realized.

The Wonder of It All

A few days between cases allowed me to travel home to the country. Sundays were usually quiet and peaceful, and this August Sunday was no exception. My father lay on the sofa reading and Uly, my brother, was doing a crossword puzzle. Uly was short for Ulysses, a name that had been cute when he was small, but now that he was approaching eighteen, it was ridiculous, for it did not seem to be in his nature to go sailing farther than the length of the nearby pond, or for adventure, farther than the village store. Aunt Mary, who kept house for us since Mother's early death, was resting in her room.

There was a knock on the kitchen door, and Mr. Morgan, a neighbour, came in. He sat down for a few minutes, but he seemed worried and fixed his gaze on me.

"Gina is sick today. She seems real bad," he said heavily. "Could you come over for a little spell until the doctor comes?"

"What seems to be the trouble, Joe?" my father asked.

Mr. Morgan shifted his cap nervously. "Well, she didn't say, only to get the doctor."

I told Mr. Morgan I would go with him.

Soon we were hurrying across the fields on a familiar path. It was a short walk, as the farms were close together. Sometimes the buildings were so close that one could imagine them calling in a friendly fashion to each other across a brook or a wooded ravine. Today, nature had kept her palette simple. The greyish-green of the woods merged into the blue haze of the distance. A pond shimmered in the sunlight and reflected a clear, blue sky. At our left, a red road wound, ribbon-like among the trees, disappeared but came into view again farther on, paler and narrowed by distance.

"It's been a great summer for pismires," Mr. Morgan observed as he looked down at the many ant hills. That was his only remark during our walk.

I knew the Morgans well, as they had been neighbours for years. Joe's wife had died, leaving him with the two girls: Georgina, twelve and Lula, nine at the time. He had managed to keep the home together. Gina was seventeen when she left home with an irresponsible young man, much against her father's wishes, and now she was back.

Their house was a small, whitewashed building with window frames and corner casings painted green. There was a small garden in front, and at the side of the house, some ducks splashed and quacked in a mud puddle.

Lula, known at school as Lool, came forward when we entered. She was fifteen now, tall, with vacuous eyes. She had been playing records on a small phonograph, but she shut it off and said pleasantly to me, "Lizzie MacRae! How are you? I hear that you are a nurse now."

"Where is Gina, Lool?" I asked, noticing that the kitchen was very hot. A pot was boiling on the stove. Suddenly, I became very alarmed. Surely this wasn't a maternity case! Oh no, surely not!

"In here," Lool said, and I followed her into the back bedroom beyond the sitting room. Lool had decorated the place with calendars from companies in Charlottetown and a gaudy motto, "God Bless Our Home." But the place was clean, and varnish glittered from the hardwood chairs. The word "Welcome" had been worked into the mat by the door, and there was embroidery on the bleached flour-bag cloth that covered the small table.

In the bedroom, I saw a changed Gina. I remembered her as she was last summer, a pretty, dark girl with plump, pink cheeks. Now she was thin, her nose sharp and pointed, and her face set in lines of pain. Yes, this was a maternity case, for there was no mistaking Gina's distress and misshapen figure.

Anxiously, I wondered if it would be of any use to send for Mrs. O'Brien, a practical nurse who lived a few miles away. But she might not be at home, and I could see that time was short. If the doctor did not come soon, I would be alone. What if something went wrong?

I called Lool into the little sitting room. "Lool, can you get clean rags, old papers and creolin? And hurry!"

The vacant look left Lool's eyes and one of fear took

its place. She said nothing but hurried out, and soon I could hear her rummaging about in an upstairs bedroom. I glanced up at the motto, "God Bless Our Home," and prayed silently, "Oh, God, don't let the baby come now!"

When Lool returned with the linen and papers, I spoke with a composure I did not feel, but if Lool could keep her head and help, all might be well. I said, "Lool, the baby is coming now, and Gina's life may depend on how well you can help. Now get me the largest apron you can find, and hurry."

Lool paled and hurried upstairs again. Soon she returned with an apron and said in a hushed, awe-struck voice, "Gina was sick all night, but she wouldn't tell anyone. Dad never wanted her to leave home. This is what she gets for not behaving herself, isn't it?"

"I don't know. Perhaps so," I answered.

"I never run the roads," Lool said, self-righteously.

"Well, perhaps that is a good thing," I said, gazing anxiously out on the dusty road, hoping I might see the doctor's car.

"I just stay home and hook mats and make quilts."

"Yes," I said as I donned a large overall apron that Lool had brought me. It was of white and blue striped material with sleeves, the stripes snaking around the arms instead of running up and down. It was long, too, with a ridiculous little frill around the hem. It was an odd garb for an obstetrician, and though I was now dressed for the case, I did not feel any more competent.

A cat came in and rubbed in a friendly way against me.

"Take the cat out, Lool," I said, knowing that Gina's pains were growing stronger.

Lool took the cat out and returned looking paler than before. "I think I'm going to vomit," she said. She sank down by the bed and I supposed she had fainted, yet I couldn't attend to her now. I had prepared my hands as well as possible for the case. "Second stage of labor," I said to myself as I stepped over Lool, now lying by the bed.

Gina moaned continuously. I looked down at my dripping hands and considered what complications I might encounter. Suppose there was a hemorrhage I couldn't control! Oh, Mercy! Suppose the cord was around the baby's neck! Well, yes, I could attend to that.

A car came up the road. It might be the doctor? But no, it wasn't the doctor. Just then Gina screamed in pain. The baby was coming now, for good or evil. With my elbow, I wiped the sweat from my forehead as I continued with my work. Before long there was the baby, kicking and crying, and Gina seemed to be all right.

Lool got up and staggered weakly out to the kitchen and I heard her announce in quick gasps to her father. "Dad, we have a baby in there, Gina's. Dad, we have a baby boy, here – now!"

But if Mr. Morgan said anything in reply, I did not hear it, and Lool said nothing more.

Gina looked up at me in an inquiring way and smiled when I told her she had a son. She was weak but well and happy, which I considered wonderful since the baby had been born without benefit of chloroform or mask, and there had been no sterile sheets, stockings or rubber gloves. We might as well have lived in a primitive age.

I went out to the kitchen feeling as if I had helped move the world. It wasn't possible not to feel some pride of accomplishment. Then I heard the doctor's car in the yard. He asked Mr. Morgan about Gina, then he asked for a stick of wood to put under a car wheel, as he had trouble getting the car stopped. He seemed relieved to hear that everything was over and after a quick inspection of the patients, left with a promise to return the following day.

I wondered what Mr. Morgan thought of all this. I had caught glimpses of him in the kitchen sitting with a bowed head, looking old and tired. Was he angry? Fathers in such circumstances usually were, but then I saw him take the baby in his arms and heard him say, "You poor little creeter." And when the baby's head fell weakly to one side he said tenderly, "Your neck is weak." He looked at the baby critically, his face transformed with sympathy. Later he went into the bedroom and I heard him talking to Gina. She said she thought she would call the baby Merle.

"Yes, yes," he said slowly, "there ain't never been anyone in our family called Merle. Where did you hear that?"

"Well, I just like the name. And I think he had better go to the orphanage; I can't expect Lool to look after him and I want to go to town to work. I'll have to earn some money, Dad."

"Oh no! You don't send him to the orphanage! We can look after him. Besides, his neck is not strong enough to go out amongst strangers."

Tears came into Gina's eyes. "Oh, Dad," she said, "We will call the baby Joseph. To heck with Merle. I am sure he should be called after you because you have always been so good to us. I will stay home if you think I should."

Lool came to watch me while I bathed the infant. "Oh, gee, ain't he small though," she said as she took a small fist in hers. The tiny fingers curled about her hand and held on. "Oh look, Lizzie, he knows I am his aunt; he is holding my hand. Ain't that cute though!"

But there were no baby clothes, and as Lool said, it took some doing to get him dressed. A sheet was torn up into diapers, then one of Lool's slips was pinned about the body. It fell like a christening robe and was topped with a white sweater with sleeves that were so long they waved about with each movement of the baby's arms. Lool was determined to have clothes made as soon as possible and to get pretty blue sweaters and booties.

I thought Lool seemed happy over the baby, and after all, he was likely to have a very good home. He would have two devoted nurses and a grandfather standing watch to see that all was well with him.

My work was finished and I was preparing to leave when Mr. Morgan said, "How much do we owe you? What is your bill?"

This was something I hadn't thought of. What money could pay for the anxiety of the afternoon? "Oh, nothing," I said. "I am not in uniform."

"Oh yes, you'd better take something," he insisted.

"Yes," Lool joined in, "take some money."

I knew they were not at all well off, yet they wanted to know I had been paid. "Would a dollar be all right?" I asked.

Mr. Morgan hurried to get the money. "That is not much for all you did," he said. I gave a last long look at the baby in a clothes basket, said goodbye, and walked home. Bright streaks coloured the western sky and the landscape had taken on the shades of evening; otherwise, nothing had changed, although much had happened since I had walked there in the early afternoon.

Uly and Father were in the kitchen when I got home. They wanted to know what Gina's trouble was, but by all the ethics of nursing, I couldn't tell them. I had a glimpse of Uly's face, wide-eyed and open-mouthed as I went upstairs. I was glad Aunt Mary had gone off to visit a neighbour. It had taken all my professional pride to stop me from running to my father and crying on his shoulder. I wanted to say, "I did it all by myself!" But I was determined that I would be considered a mature person, and as I lay on the white coverlet of my bed, exhausted, tears ran out of the corners of my eyes, unchecked, as I thought of the wonder of it all.

She Had Her Dignity,
Did Mrs. O'Brien

I had another case before I went back to my rooming house. I was returning from a walk to the river when I saw two men hurrying towards me. One began to yell "Hello" and wave his arms. I hurried towards them and they hurried towards me, as if in a pantomime, until I was within earshot. I heard, "Can you come? The doctor needs you at Smith's house, Miss MacRae." I was too surprised then to wonder why two men had come with the message. We got into the car that they had left in our yard and hurried up the long hill to Josiah Smith's house.

It was another maternity case. The commotion was caused by Mrs. Smith's labour coming three weeks early. I might have known from the excited appearance of the messengers and their admonitions to make haste. Men cannot get used to the two great events of this life: the coming in and the going out, I mused. Men have lived on this planet for centuries and yet are no more composed when a birth takes place today than they were at the start. Science has discussed ways and has evolved tables and sterile instruments to be used, and many books have been written as to what is best and what is not. But no book has been written on how to keep cool when going for a doctor or a nurse. Later I saw Mr. Smith leave in a terrible rush to get Mrs. O'Brien, the practical nurse who lived a few miles away.

About the yard was a scene of suspended activity where the threshing machine had been stopped at midday. I thought, no wonder the poor woman took to her bed. I noticed that the yard was filled with trucks, cars, and machinery, and the kitchen was filled with the threshing crew having their midday dinner. The Fuller Brush man also came in at the height of the activity. He was passing through, and seeing the gathering, thought he might have a very good opportunity to make sales!

As I made the necessary preparations, I felt the curious eyes upon me each time I went into the kitchen. I was wearing a huge, gathered apron that had been given to me to wear over my light summer dress. I began to sterilize bundles of linen which looked like loaves of bread as I popped them into the oven. Mrs. Smith's mother presided over the gathering in the kitchen and introduced me to each of the men.

"Pleased to meet you," they said politely, and they all rose in turn to shake my hand. At that time, the door opened and Mrs. O'Brien came in. She was a stout, florid woman, dressed in older style skirts, and a light straw hat with two tassels that moved importantly as she was introduced to the company. One of the men brought in her two suitcases, a very large one and a smaller one of black leather with her name in gold letters,

MRS. CECILIA O'BRIEN.

Mrs. Smith's mother asked me to take Mrs. O'Brien upstairs and show her the room where she would sleep next to the patient. As we walked upstairs, Mrs. O'Brien said in her broad Irish brogue, "Glory be to God, Nurse, I thought I'd be killed, the way that man took us over the roads! He was in such a tear. Once he had to stop for water for the car, running over to the pond and all the way back. I never seen the likes of such rushing!"

Soon Dr. Ryan came puffing up the stairs. I had known him from my childhood as a blustering, kind, hard-working doctor. I felt that he was looking his helpers over, Mrs. O'Brien in a polka-dotted dress and myself in the flowing white apron.

When he went to scrub up, I walked behind him, and looking up at the broad back, I was thankful. The doctor was now between me and all the forces of death and destruction, not at all as it has been at the Morgan's home.

When the child was born and had uttered its first cry, there was something elemental in Mrs. O'Brien's appearance. Her face was transformed by a look of exultation. "Glory be to God," she exclaimed in a reverent tone and snatched up the baby. When we heard again that loud, hoarse cry, Mrs. O'Brien tried to soothe it by a motion known as "jiggling," disapproved of by the professionals. But Mrs. O'Brien was in a transport of happiness and beyond noticing the doctor's frown of displeasure.

When the doctor had left and the exhausted mother was sleeping, I prepared to bath the baby. "Glory be, are you wearing a mask, then?" she inquired, and when I nodded in the affirmative, she said, "But the baby can't see you!" I was too preoccupied to consider the logic of her remark, but she talked on jovially, telling of cases she had and of certain ones that had gone to a hospital. She mentioned the latter ones with a sigh, and I felt that she did not greatly approve. Her cases were usually attended to at home, and she took pride in her accomplishments and her reputation as a seasoned nurse.

She talked fast, without waiting for breath, except for a sharp intake at inconvenient times. "I had a letter from the County Line man's wife. She said, 'I'm pregnant and what can you do about it?' She always says that when she wants me to nurse her. I been with her five times and you shoulda seen the last baby! It was the prettiest thing you ever saw. She had convulsion fits the last time and I guess she's afraid she'll have them again. She said, 'Come, Mrs. O'Brien, and bring your couterments with you'. She's an awful nice woman."

"What accoutrements have you, Mrs. O'Brien?" I asked, for I had come to the case with nothing.

"Well, I have things for the baby, mostly, in this suitcase," she said, and opened it for inspection.

I saw a large bottle of Gripe, which I knew to be a mild soothing syrup, a pacifier named Infant's Delight, a square of brightly-coloured oilcloth, some scorched clothes, an infant's syringe, a bottle of goose grease, and a box of toothpicks, which Mrs. O'Brien explained were mint-flavored. She told me how good the goose grease was for patients with bronchitis. "It's the best," she said. "You can rub it on the chest, shoulders, and back, and then give them some to swallow – to stop the coughing." Her manner was almost conspiratorial as she let me in on the secrets of her trade.

Then she looked suspiciously at a cup of absorbent cotton in boiled water. "What's them things in the cup?" she asked.

"These are for the baby's mouth and eyes."

"Well," she said with a toss of her head, – she had her dignity, did Mrs. O'Brien – "I never touch the baby's mouth because I'm afraid of thrush. A baby in Marshfield died of thrush."

"Yes, but we use a treatment to prevent that. You see, thrush is caused by a germ, so we boil everything, including the nipples and pacifiers, if we use them," I said.

Mrs. O'Brien gave me a skeptical glance. "I've looked after a lot of babies, and I had two of me own. One died when it was just two days, of jaunders, and before the next one came, Patrick O'Brien went off to New Brunswick to work in the woods and I never heard of him after. I put an ad in the paper to see if he would answer. I made it up exactly like it went in. It said he had one squint eye and a purple birthmark on his neck, worse in blueberry time. It said to get in touch with his wife because she had news for him – a new baby. But I never got a line! Then my little girl died, so I'm alone now." She paused for breath, sighing, her eyes moist, and went on quickly as if to stifle the sad thought, "I thought Patrick might have gone to Halifax or Montreal to get his birthmark taken off. But it might have come off anyway, cause I used to rub it with a silver spoon and a brooch with two little hearts on it that he gave me before we was married. Now, you're not goin' to leave the feet loose like that, are you? He'll kick them booties off in no time," Mrs. O'Brien expostulated indignantly, looking at the baby's feet.

Since our discussion on my novel ways seemed to be getting nowhere, she appeared to change the subject. "What do you nurses have that black band on your cap for?" she asked.

"Graduate nurses wear them to distinguish them from the students."

"Oh, I thought you were in mournin' for somebody, maybe a patient you'd lost, or something," she said with a slight sniff.

Now that the baby had arrived and both mother and child were doing well, I made plans to leave. Mrs. O'Brien would stay on until Mrs. Smith was strong enough to take over her normal household tasks. Since this was Mrs. O'Brien's case, she could manage as she pleased now, but I felt sure there would be no boiling of pacifiers or nipples.

At home, my Aunt Mary inquired about Mrs. Smith. "Now, Mrs. O'Brien will do better than you," she said, "because a trained nurse can't do the housework that Mrs. O'Brien is used to doing." Apparently, Aunt Mary still thought of me as a young flapper, only good for lying on the sofa and reading novels!

She continued, "I was talking to Phemy Blatch about nurses because she got one when her seventh child was born. The trouble was that the nurse didn't care for cooking. She just wanted to look after Phemy and the baby. So Phemy's husband, Brooges, had to do all the cooking. Lucky thing he had just killed a beef. But he had to look after the other children, too, poor soul. Well, it was so hard on Phemy thinking of poor Brooges having to cook the beefsteak and help with the children and do all the barn work, that she couldn't rest a-tall! So when her next child was born, did she get a trained nurse? No, she didn't. She got a woman like Mrs. O'Brien that cooked and did housework too." Having delivered herself of these thoughts on the new-fangled ways of the nursing profession, Aunt Mary sat back in her rocker with a satisfied expression.

"Yes," I ventured, "but trained nurses do more for the patients, Aunt Mary. I am sure they get better care."

"I don't know about that." My aunt compressed her lips as she always did when displeased. Why was she so old-fashioned and provincial in regard to registered nurses? She hadn't wanted me to leave home or take up nursing as a profession. Perhaps there was some underlying fear for me. She had had a younger sister, my Aunt Louisa, who had trained as a nurse and had gone to the South Seas to do missionary work. She had died there under suspicious circumstances. Aunt Mary had taken the news of her death very hard and had said often with bitterness that she had died among foreigners and had been denied a Christian burial. I sometimes wondered what the "circumstances" could have been. A terrible thought came into my head that maybe she had been eaten by cannibals.

Despite my aunt's critical attitude, I realized it was concern for my welfare that led her to take a hard line against nursing. She probably thought that if she disapproved strongly, I would give it up, come home, and marry one of the neighbourhood farmers.

But the war had changed the lives of women forevermore. They had been working in war industries, nursing at the front lines of battle, and were even talking about voting. Things would never be the same for any of us.

I See You, You Big Bloke!

Back in Brighton after the weekend at home, I was enjoying my morning tea when the phone rang. Dr. Grant was on the line, his voice gruff and coolly impersonal. "Miss. MacRae, will you come to 37 Weston Street tomorrow at nine? It is a slight operation, just opening an abscess. It is a child."

"Yes, Dr. Grant, I'll be there." I hung up the phone and sat thinking about Dr. Grant and his attitude towards the nurses as trainees. Would he treat a graduate nurse with more respect? Martin had said that she was learning to assume an authoritative manner as to be ready for private duty. I thought perhaps I lacked this manner but hoped for the best.

I fell asleep thinking of this, but I awoke before midnight. I had had a dream, ridiculously silly, in which Dr. Grant was in the act of cleaning our kitchen at home and was hanging up four kitchen towels for a screen for an operation that was to take place at once. Sometimes the patient seemed to be myself, sometimes my father, while my aunt directed the whole performance in her best authoritative manner!

I lay awake thinking of the case. I wondered if the child would be frightened. In our nursing manual, there had been a picture of a nurse restraining a child, but in the picture, there was no crying, no kicking, no flailing of arms, no dishevelled nurse with beady eyes, no angry doctor, and no distraught mother in the background. Lavinia Dock, who wrote advice for nurses, must have been an idealist.

The following morning, I found the number of the very shabby house. The doctor was waiting for me. He stood leaning against an old piano, tall and dark with his usual expression, which I considered cranky. "Prepare the area," he said, the minute I stepped into the room. I glanced at my watch and was pleased to see it was not yet nine o'clock. As I went about my preparations, I remembered that at the nurses' dance he had told me that my eyes were very blue and my hair very black; but that was unimportant, as I cared little for his opinion.

Jimmy, the patient, was six years old. His face was flushed and his tongue showed through the vacancies in his front teeth. He crushed the thin blanket around him and said through clenched teeth, "You leave me alone!" He was not very tractable and "You leave me alone" seemed to be his whole vocabulary. His mother, a mild, ineffectual-looking woman came forward to help. "Jimmy, be a good boy and let the nurse fix you up," she said.

I went into the kitchen and found Nettie, a young girl who had been called in to mind the other children. Six noisy children were playing under and around the long kitchen table, and she was unsuccessfully trying to keep order.

"Could you get me a basin that I could use for a disinfectant solution, please?" I asked.

Nettie rushed to the cupboard and produced a slightly rusted bake pan and a dishpan which had a small hole plugged by a rag. I had a choice, but it was hard to choose. The doctor might rage, but I picked the dishpan. Then I got boiling water from the big kettle on the stove and hastened back to the parlour with it, through the milling children.

"You may give him his hypo now, Nurse," Dr. Grant said as he energetically scrubbed his hands.

But when I came forward with the hypo, Jimmy drew back in fear. He covered his head with the blanket and then, finding a convenient hole, he looked out through it at the doctor. "I see you, you big bloke," he growled. "You are going to stab me!"

"Look here, Jim," the doctor said, coming forward with dripping hands, "We are not going to hurt you. Now be a good boy and it will be much easier."

"Yes, you are going to hurt me. Take away that needle thing!"

The doctor picked him up.

"You stop that, you dirty brute!" Jimmy shouted.

Dr. Grant ignored his tantrum and carried him, kicking, over to the table. "Give him a little of this," he said as he put a bottle and a mask into my hand.

The mask was hardly over his nose when Jimmy caught it and sent it flying across the room. I made a dash for the mask and noticed that Dr. Grant seemed to be taking all the fuss and confusion rather well, not his usual pattern.

Jimmy's mother came in and repeated, "Now Jimmy, be a good boy."

Finally, with our combined efforts, Jimmy was put to sleep. It did not take long to open the abscess. Just a few seconds and the dreaded business was over and Jimmy was carried back to his bed.

I was tidying up the room when Jimmy opened his eyes and unexpectedly smiled at me. Dr. Grant had taken off his gown and was preparing to leave. He stood looking thoughtfully at Jimmy who had called out for a glass of water. "Get him some ice to suck," Dr. Grant said. "He hasn't had enough ether to upset him. I think we may leave now that he is fully conscious. I'm going your way, Nurse, if you care to come now."

"Thank you, Doctor," I said and looked at the boy's mother who had said she would get the ice. Her eyes were reddened, and her hair hung in untidy wisps about her face. No doubt this had been an ordeal for her.

"Goodbye, Jimmy," I said. "Goodbye," he answered and smiled again.

As we drove to my rooming house in Dr. Grant's shiny new automobile, he remarked, "That child was hard to handle. I wouldn't want to have too much to do with him, would you?"

"Yes, he was pretty naughty," I said. Yet I wondered if the doctor didn't act in much the same way when he was displeased. I remembered the time I had come across some nurses working in Number Four. They were painstakingly scraping Plaster of Paris off a wall, where Dr. Grant had thrown it in a rage. It seemed that it hadn't been properly mixed for a cast he was making, and in his anger, he splashed it about.

I glanced up at the doctor as he sat with his eyes on the road. His serious profile reminded me of a picture I had seen of an old Roman coin embossed with the head of Julius Caesar.

He turned and looked at me intently. He said, "Where do you intend to nurse, now that you are through? Here on the Island, I hope?"

"I suppose I will go on nursing around the country and in the hospital," I replied.

"That is right," he said approvingly. "There is enough nursing here on the Island if you will stay. The trouble is, the nurses go off to the United States and other places. I have a case right now that may need nursing care. It is a sore throat and I quarantined the family because I feared scarlet fever. I thought the child had a strawberry tongue, but sometimes it's hard to tell. Might be from the stomach," he said as if thinking aloud.

Now we were coming to the outskirts of Victoria Park, where tall spruce trees lined the driveway. I looked up at the treetops and remarked irrelevantly, "I wonder if there is any gum on those trees. Have you ever picked gum off spruce trees, Dr. Grant?"

"Oh yes, long ago," he answered, smiling. "I used to pick gum and chew it when I was a child."

Then he returned to his previous mental groove and added, "We get a lot of medicine from the trees. The eucalyptus tree, which is called the blue gum tree, supplies tannic acid and oil of eucalyptus from the leaves." He lapsed again into gloomy meditation. "That man Dawson in the ward is pretty sick. I ordered hot dressings for him and I hope he won't be neglected," he continued.

"I think the nurses will look after him all right," I said. He gave a doubtful look and I thought, Oh, what's the use of saying anything! He has already made up his mind as to the treatment they will receive. I admired Dr. Grant but wished he would acknowledge all the good that nurses provided to their patients.

We were at the water's edge and a very refreshing breeze came to us. Across the blue, sunny water, the sound of boats could be heard. Some carefree people were sitting on a wharf, some were bathing, and others sat on the grass watching their children at play. This is the prettiest part of the city, I thought. Anyone could be happy here at Brighton.

And perhaps the happy scene did work as an alchemy on Dr. Grant's mood, because a few minutes later when he left me at my door, he smiled pleasantly and said, "Well, be seeing you, Miss MacRae."

Dr. Grant put his hand on the car door just as a stray gust of wind tore forcibly at his hat. He clutched at it quickly. This was a good thing. Nature just didn't play tricks on Dr. Grant. He was too dignified to encounter any playful pranks. Dr. Burke, yes, he was usually laughing, and Dr. MacLeod wouldn't have minded. He was a little more mellow and accustomed to the unpredictable ways of nature.

After a simple dinner in my room, I sat by the window and thought of nursing and of Dr. Grant. He was unreasonable at times, but if I were very ill, I supposed I should want Dr. Grant as a doctor. He gave his patients assurance by his very concern over their condition. As if he said, "Yes, heart, body, and soul, I am in this trouble with you." That was why his office was usually filled to overflowing while other doctors had fewer patients than they wished.

Buy a Fish?

The sand at Rustico beach is hard and firm, bare of seaweed, stones, or strange looking minute fish found on the nearby sands. The great surge of the Atlantic had washed them away. It would also wash away the many small buildings the fishermen had for their work if they had not been placed high on stilts. The hotel, some places of business, and the dwellings had been built cautiously away at a distance, safe from the menacing, roaring waves. But even with this precaution, there was often much destruction in man against nature, and nature often won. Traps were washed away, buildings torn down, ships sunk, and the ocean, angrily showing what she could do, tossed the debris about the shore.

But today as I walked on the firm sand, nature smiled and was congenial. There was no sign of great waves, only ripples, white-crested, came to my feet then apologetically receded. The sun shone in a warm, comfortable way, with no blinding or scorching rays thrown out to tire or weaken. September was at her best today, beautiful but insincere, since we could not depend on her warmth for long.

The fishing boats were returning. Men were busy on the wharves, some running in preparation for the coming in of the boats, while the gulls followed, flew overhead, swooped down and screeched in hungry expectation. Soon the cleanings of fish would be thrown out.

I was on a case here in one of the dwellings. One of the fishermen had become very ill. Although typhoid was rarely found now, still the doctor had said, "Yes, definitely typhoid." Typhoid could be cared for in the homes if a trained nurse was in charge. And it must not spread. This required much caution. Separate dishes, bedding and the use of disinfectants; chloride of lime and Lysol were used. In spite of using hand lotion, my hands grew red and rough with the technique: touch patient, touch bedding or dishes – disinfect hands.

I returned to a pretty white-painted cottage where sweet peas grew by the front walk. Monique, my patient's sister, who had spelled me off, rose to meet me. She was a dark, pretty girl in her teens who now looked sad – "Tony was so sick, mon Dieu. Did you have a nice walk, Nurse?" she asked me.

"Yes, lovely. Did you remember about your hands, Monique? Did you disinfect them?"

"Yes, I disinfect, but Tony, he not know me when I speak. I call loud, see if he look. No, no look," she shook her head mournfully.

"No, he is too sick to notice, but in the mornings, he is brighter before the fever becomes too high; he talks sometimes. He is no worse."

I had been on the case a week now. Monique and her father had relieved me so that I got some sleep and a walk in the fresh air each day. But I hoped for a change. I wished the temperature would go down, but every afternoon it returned, and I tried to provide comfort with a tepid sponge. The doctor's visit hadn't been encouraging. Tony had been muttering and picking at the bedclothes when he saw him. The picking at the bedclothes was always a serious symptom.

Tony had helped his father with the fishing and had gone with wagonloads of fish, selling from door to door, and now sometimes in delirium, he would look up at me and ask me to buy a fish. Sometimes he seemed to be imploring me to buy. Perhaps he felt that he had had a poor day and this was his last chance.

"Yes, yes, I'll buy one. I'll buy more than one."

But these words could not break through his dull maze of thought. He was in a confused state of delirium where the mind goes round and round, unhappily like an old refrain, never changing, never coming to any definite conclusion, for he soon said again, "Buy a fish?"

Tony's mother came in and looked anxiously toward the bed. She was short and dark with shoulders a bit rounded. Her black hair was drawn tightly back from a face becoming a bit wrinkled. Her housedress, belted at the waist, revealed a figure that hadn't regained its normal shape after the bearing of many children.

"I have the tomato that I ripened in an old sack behind the stove. Could Tony eat one?" she asked and went on, "And here is a bottle of wine that his cousin, Jim LeClerc, brought him. But be careful if you open it. It foments over the cloth."

"Oh no, I am afraid he can't take much yet but milk and water. He can't have anything solid to eat; and the wine, it will keep until he is better."

They were anxious to do something for him and felt helpless. They could do nothing but wait.

Tony had many cousins, all thin and dark like himself. They all wanted to see Tony and all expressed their kinship by bearing gifts. Clams, oysters, vegetables, and berries to make a jam to spread on the bread were all offered, but poor Tony, sometimes able to nod a grateful, "thank you," could take nothing.

Every afternoon, Tony's grandfather, Mr. Gallant, came to look in on him. The old man was very badly crippled with arthritis. Bent over and leaning on two canes and usually dressed in a long black coat, he was not unlike a large, black beetle. The first day, he had looked doubtfully at Tony but cautiously backed out to the sitting room. "It is catching, isn't it?"

"You have to take the germ by mouth. If you touch dishes or anything of Tony's, wash your hands. We have a disinfectant here for hands."

Mr. Gallant waved aside the rocking chair, laid by his canes and eased himself down to a straight, hard chair.

"Better for me," he said. He smiled and began to eulogize Tony. "He was always a good boy. He not go to make spree, get drunk, get girls in trouble, lose money with cards, have accident…he stay and fish and help his father. He never – what you say? complain." And now when he thought of him so sick it was too much. Some tears dropped and he did not bother to wipe them away.

"How are you feeling yourself, Mr. Gallant?" I asked.

"I am well only for this rheumatics. I stay too long in cold water. I work out too much in cold damp. Now I crippled. But fishing good now. Canning factories come, good help. My son Peter awful smart man, make the money here. Once thought to go into politics. He be nominated for parliament. Nobody beat him, but he stay home." I noticed he looked towards the door often. Peter would soon be coming home to supper.

But Maria, Tony's older sister who was employed at the hotel, came first. She went in at once to see Tony, but he was too ill to notice her smile. She was pretty, with dark hair curled down to her shoulders. She was wearing a simple white dress, and as she took up an empty jug, I thought of a picture by one of the old masters, "Girl with Pitcher." She looked very sad. "He is just the same, no better." She looked at me, "Has he been like that all day?"

"Yes, pretty much the same. But he has times when he is quite conscious."

Everyone at suppertime felt the spell of Tony's sickness. It was like a pall. Any remark on any subject, even a bright one, only brought up the thought of Tony. Mr. Peter

Gallant, Tony's father, wondered if there would be an election this fall. No need of it, the current government was doing well. He was thankful that all his family felt as he did and that they were always strong Liberals since Laurier. But poor Tony, now so low, might never live to vote again.

"I gave the house a good cleaning today," Monique said, "and the walls and pictures washed for fly specks, but tonight after supper we must scrub. We are sure to have a lot of company, tomorrow being Sunday, and Mother baked all day for lunches tonight and supper tomorrow. She has three cakes and cookies and two pies. With the fish and crackers and cheese, perhaps enough."

"I think Alphonse and all of them might come tomorrow if they heard about Tony, and they have a car now. He is my brother in Charlottetown, and he has a large family," Mrs. Gallant turned to me to explain.

"But would they all stay to supper?" I asked.

"Oh, yes, I would not like them to leave here hungry. We never do let anyone go away hungry. Even if Tony's sick, we must do as well as we can." Then she added, "Nothing matters if Tony gets better."

I looked up at the clean, white wall, the glittering glass on the picture of the Sacred Heart, the baking visible on the cupboard, all done in preparation for the coming Sabbath.

We finished our supper of Digby herring, hard, kneaded biscuits, cookies, jam and many cups of strong tea.

Sunday was fine, the weather perfect, the prognosis for visitors good. Monique and Maria, dressed in dainty pink and blue dresses, walked down past the sweet peas, looking like overgrown flowers themselves. A gust of ocean breeze tugged at their small straw hats. They snatched at them quickly. They were on their way to Mass. They must walk as they had no car as yet, but they hoped their father would get one soon. It was a piece to walk all right, but nothing was too hard now. Like penance, it might help poor Tony. They wouldn't neglect any religious duties. Prayers would be freely offered. Candles lit and money paid. They would ask Father Malone what they could do.

In the afternoon, when I had returned from my walk, I saw that Monique and Maria had pinned a cross on Tony. It was about five inches long in a dull metal finish. But Tony was alert enough to notice. He objected, "Too much trouble for the nurse, pin on, pin off all time." This brought the sisters to me. Would I mind the pinning and taking off? No, I wouldn't mind anything that gave them comfort. They believed the cross could help. Surely the gentle Jesus would look down, remember his own suffering, and pity a poor mortal, especially one who had faith enough to wear a crucifix. So the cross remained.

But that day Father Malone came to anoint Tony for death. The family had wished for the last rites. It would be best in case Tony took worse suddenly and passed away unprepared. Think of the worry and unhappiness. "You don't really think he will get better, do you?" the priest asked me, as he saw how alarmed I had become.

"Yes, I think he may get better. The disease will run its course. I think if you anoint, he will become discouraged and not fight anymore."

"You Protestants don't seem to realize the seriousness of death. Your attitude seems to be that it doesn't matter, one way or another. Surely not many are holy enough to meet God."

I looked up at Father Malone, there was nothing cadaverous about him. He seemed very large with much flesh and blood, for I had been looking long at the emaciated Tony. I knew nothing I could say would change Father Malone in his course of action. I did not have an authoritative manner. My appearance just then could command little respect, in a uniform done up in the kitchen with sad irons which were sad enough that they left a black streak on the white linen. Would a General get instant obedience if it were not for a uniform with gold braid and brass buttons?

"Yes, Father Malone, I do understand a bit, but you see, for days and nights now I have been trying to keep a door closed so that Death might not enter. It seems to me that you are trying to open that door."

"Oh no, Nurse. What I am going to do won't alter his physical condition. The last rites have been known to help the patient many times to regain health I assure you," Then he added, "I may not do it all today," as he went in to see Tony.

Monique and I sat together in the sitting room. We could hear some preparation. We heard the words, "In the name of the Father and of the Son and of the Holy Ghost." I saw that Monique was crying and tears came to my own eyes. The door was now wide open.

When Father Malone had gone, I went in to encourage him if I could. "You are doing all right, Tony. You are going to get better," and surprisingly, Tony understood and nodded his head.

That evening, the company came in noiselessly. They had tea, talked in low voices and left softly, closing the door behind them. They had pity and respect for the Gallants in their trouble. And the priest had come. They felt the awe of death. "Holy Mary, Mother of God, pray for us sinners, and pray for Tony that he may get well," I heard the family saying the Rosary.

I thought at times during the night that Tony was better, but then he began again to mutter about fish.

Alphonse and "all of them" came. They had only just heard of the illness. Soon the kitchen and living room seemed to be filled. Alphonse was a large, stout man, and his wife, not too small herself, came in with their ten children. Seven little boys in trousers with braces stood before me like an army of little men. The girls came too. They were younger, all very round-eyed. They were all quiet, as I imagined they had been warned.

Mrs. Alphonse was a pleasant-faced, cheerful woman, and if a prize had been given for efficiency, it would have been hers.

"How could you dress so many and get them ready to come?" I asked her.

"Oh, it wasn't so bad. Alphonse helped me and Pierre is old enough to help with the younger ones."

"You have ten?" I had counted them.

"Yes, that's enough," she said and smiled. "But I wouldn't want to part with any of them." Then looking very serious, she said,

"Too bad about Tony. A nice boy, Tony."

Monique came with cookies for the children, and the ten gathered around the long kitchen table munching happily.

There was an aura of death surrounding Tony that seemed to attract the curious. I told them, "When he is a bit better, you can see him," or "he is sleeping," or often, "he is unconscious, he won't know you." But when Alphonse and his wife came to me, I knew they couldn't be turned away.

"We won't go in. We'll just look in at the door," Mrs. Alphonse said.

There was Tony, isolated in a big bed, his dark colouring accentuated by the whiteness of the sheets. His trembling hands busy with the bedding, his muttering, his flushed face and closed eyes, all added to their fears.

After standing watching for a few minutes, they turned away sadly. They liked Tony.

"Today we went for clams," Alphonse said in a low voice, "Could he eat them?"

"No, but perhaps I might strain out some. He could drink the milk of the stew. He can only take liquids."

The roar of the ocean came from the open window. It was not a comforting sound. Now it suggested the immensity of nature, menacing and unkind. A foghorn sounded as if in protest.

But later that evening, Tony's temperature had not risen so high, and I put a lower dot on the chart. It showed quite a decline. Monique came in to sit with him for a while and she smiled and looked encouraged when I told her of his temperature.

The clock ticked away the seconds, the minutes, the days.

A week later, Maria brought the news to the hotel that Tony was better. The proprietor was pleased. He was worried that the disease might spread because of Maria working in the hotel restaurant. He must not mention the word typhoid. He had an unhappy mental vision of all the guests packing and going out the door.

Maria rushed around being generally helpful. Today, she did not mind if the guests were unreasonable, demanding strange things. The brilliants in her tortoiseshell comb twinkled happily. Her small heels beat a tattoo on the tiled floor, and when a guest complained that she hadn't slept well, Maria only responded with a broad grin. She couldn't make the sad face this morning, even if the woman didn't sleep.

Now that Tony was better, the cousins all came. They were musical. One of them, Andre, had won a prize for violin playing at a contest, and if Tony wished, Andre and the other cousins would play some music for him. Tony did want the music. It might help him forget the awful emptiness of his stomach. He was hungry, and he could still only have small amounts of food.

Somebody had played a trick on Andre. When he took his violin to play, pressed the bow and lifted his foot to keep time, no sound came from the strings. Somebody had greased the strings. "So you wouldn't be playing when Tony was dying," said his brother. But the music began a bit later, and the song, "Hallelujah, I'm a Bum!" rang out. The "Hallelujah," in the ribald song, perhaps expressed their joy. Monique played the organ and sang some French songs. She, too, was musical and she felt like singing.

"I can't remember for such a long time when I was sick," Tony said when the concert was over. "Did I say anything? Did I talk?"

"Yes, you did."

"Nothing bad, I hope. Did I swear?"

"No, nothing bad. You were only asking me to buy a fish."

"I wanted you to buy a fish, Nurse? You must have laughed!"

"No, I didn't laugh. That talking goes with delirium or sometimes when the mind has been drugged. I had a friend who repeated Robert Service's poems both going under and coming out of the anesthetic. You know, "The Cremation of Sam McGee.""

I was taking my last walk on the beach for I was leaving tomorrow. To the northwest was Anne Country, Cavendish, with all its glamour, its Lake of Shining Waters, its Lovers' Lane, its fields, its Haunted Wood, its sand dunes and the wide expanse of firm sand. To the east was South Rustico, where fishing was carried out on a smaller scale. There, at the end of the winding road was the convent school, a seat of learning where both Catholics and Protestants mingled for higher erudition, the big brick church to which many walked long distances but were not un-wearied because of their zeal and a belief in spiritual help.

Now it lay in a mist, only outlines of distant houses and banks visible in a greyish-blue colouring which artists had found almost impossible to copy. Before me were the fishing boats, and something else, a large vessel offshore but near enough for the rowing out of boats and the giving off some of its cargo. It was a rumrunner. I watched idly while a smaller boat approached it quickly. Broad daylight! But there were no police boats around today. I was thankful that the Gallant home had not been that of a bootlegger. It was possible to tell which homes in the village were selling the illicit liquor – those which had their storm doors on all summer, with little glass panes to look out and warn of approaching Mounties!

I had heard some stories whispered in the Gallant kitchen of the rum-running trade. They laughed at the discomfiture of one bootlegger whose store of liquor was stolen. He couldn't very well go to the Mounties to complain but had to suffer the loss.

Now that my time with these good people was over, a neighbour who owned a car would take me home, and when goodbyes were said and good wishes exchanged, I was on my way.

When we reached the bridge, the tide was out. A few people, men, with trouser-legs tucked up and women, skirts lifted high and caught at the waistband, were digging clams. A red bank bordered by spruce, and a maple tree, whose leaves were already turning yellow and red, showed vividly bright in the afternoon sun. Beyond were the farm-lands, there was the yellow of harvested grain crops, the red of newly turned soil of the potato fields and the faded tint of the grass around the fields. Lombardy poplars grew along a driveway with spaced precision, throwing patches of shade across the red soil.

At home, nothing had changed. "How are you feeling, Aunt Mary?" I inquired.

"Fine, but a bit tired. We were picking the winter apples yesterday. It is a tiresome job, and I am not as young as I once was."

I went out to see the flowers: petunias, marigolds, phlox and alyssum tangled with a clematis vine, trailing and growing about the window where Aunt Mary's potted geraniums were peeping out. The moonflower vines, twined around the verandah post, had many blossoms too shy and delicate to open to the bright light of day, but like the glow-worm, they gave cheer and beauty to the night. Sadly, it would not be long before the first frost would take them and a new season would begin.

Leakerage of the Heart

It was a day to be thankful for. The sun glistened on bril-liant leaves of red and gold, and across the river, the woods and hills were enveloped in a bluish-green mist, the haze of autumn. A robin sang out joyfully from a nearby tree as I entered the yard of a house situated next to a beautiful birch grove. But there was little joy inside the comfortable family home. A tall, thin woman in her early thirties met me at the door. Her tired, bloodshot eyes were dull and without expression, her shoulders drooped with weariness, and when she took me to the upstairs spare room, there was no spring or lightness in her step. Loss of sleep and worry robbed her of her vitality.

"I am Bob's mother," she said. "And I am glad you were able to come to us. Bob is very sick and we have to face it, he may not get better. He took sick about a week ago with a sore throat, but we never thought of diphtheria until we got the doctor. He gave him a dose of antitoxin, so we were up all last night. I'll take you in when you are ready," she said wearily.

I changed into my uniform and walked down the hall to my patient's room. I lifted a sheet drenched with a disinfectant, then I realized the doctor was there. He was a large, serious-faced man, and his anxiety over the patient prevented any of the formalities.

The patient, Bob Spencer, a boy of about twelve, was in great distress and was supported by a tall, thin man I supposed was the child's father. The boy was gasping, showing that little air was passing through the swollen throat. If something was not done quickly, he would smother.

"Is there anything you can do, Doctor?" the father asked. "He can't stand this much longer."

"Yes," the doctor replied, "I think I can help him."

But the boy could not bear to lie in bed. He stumbled about the room in agony, and I felt I could do little to help. This doctor had a country practice, where the harsh realities of life had seldom been blunted by the convenience and companionship of the hospital. He had faced death and birth many times, so he had toughened. He would know what had to be done, and I saw him prepare quickly to do a tracheotomy.

He took a sterile scalpel from an instrument case, and while I supported the patient, he made a swift, sure incision, cutting through the thin covering of the larynx. Air rushed into empty lungs and the patient fell back, completely relieved and in a state of apathy.

But I swayed dizzily, feeling weak and nauseated. I

staggered to a sofa at the end of the room and fell upon it. I felt ashamed. In the hospital, a patient swathed in sterile sheets and under ether seemed to lose some of his identity as a human being, but here, where the doctor had worked without benefit of ether, it was unnerving.

Feeling stronger, I went over and saw that he had clipped the wound open with sterilized hairpins. I was to hold the hairpins in place to keep the wound open in the throat, in lieu of a tracheotomy tube. The doctor explained that the tube he had used had been lost. Until he came back the next day, this was all he could do.

After the doctor had given a large dose of antitoxin, he hurried away, leaving the patient to me. His father relieved me when the long monotonous hours of holding the hairpins in place became unendurable.

When daylight came, I considered the appearance of my patient. Although pale, he seemed a healthy pallor; his eyes were brighter, but his temperature continued quite high. There was an angry redness around the wound in the throat. Infection, I thought, as I applied hot compresses. But this danger, too, seemed to pass. That evening, the doctor came with the tube, so the nursing care became much easier, and because of the boy's steady improvement, happiness radiated through the house.

As my patient grew stronger, I noticed that he looked at me in a curious, reserved sort of way. Sometimes he seemed to be afraid of me. He was very polite and always addressed me as Nurse and answered my questions with, "Yes, Ma'am" and "No, Ma'am," as if I were a dignified personage. This attitude was explained partially while his mother visited him, for I heard him say, "She ain't cranky, Mom." I thought this over and assumed he had heard that nurses were disagreeable.

Bob had said little during his illness, but I knew he was thinking and I sometimes wondered what was at the back of that silence. Now he started to talk in a rush of boyish enthusiasm, his voice just beginning to quaver.

"Boy, are you fond of washing me! You washed me last night with warm soapy water and now you are at it again. Are you ever fond of soap and water!" He looked down at his bleached hands, for he had never seen them look so clean and white. "I plan to skip some washes if I ever get out of bed, and it looks now as if I might. I'd like to see Whip, my dog. And I'd like to go out and climb the red apple tree. It seems awful nice now to think I'll be able to climb that tree again!"

I told Bob that we were going to fumigate the house. Although cleanliness and sunshine were helpful to get rid of germs, the doctor and Mr. Spencer had decided on getting formaldehyde candles to burn in the rooms.

"You see, Bob, I shall fumigate parts of the house, then everybody must take a bath and wash their hair with a mild disinfectant and put clean clothing on. We shall go to the fumigated part downstairs, then I'll light candles in these rooms."

"Yes, Ma'am."

"And I must give you a shampoo," I said. "We don't want any more cases, do we?"

"No Ma'am."

I pulled out drawers and hung out clothing in the sun, dogged by the thought of the longevity of the diphtheritic germ. But when it came to lighting the candles, I felt happier, for they seemed to be beacons of hope that the dreaded disease would not strike again in this house.

Now Bob was united with the other members of the family, and Whip pounced upon him in such an ecstasy that he clung to the doorknob for support.

Mr. Spencer laughed and teased Bob about having an offer for the dog. "I can get twenty dollars for him, or even more," he said.

"But he is not for sale," Bob said as he threw the dog a piece of buttered bread.

This was a case that had turned out happily, and I left with a feeling that all was well. The dark side of nursing was in caring for those who did not make it back to health. But in Bob's case, there was nothing but joy.

That day, I met Mrs. O'Brien in a drug store. She spoke and smiled in a friendly way. She was wearing a hat trimmed with fur that formed a border around her pink and white unwrinkled face, and I thought she looked not unlike a grownup baby. She hurried to tell me that she was in Charlottetown for the day and that she had had a very important case. A Mr. Stalkwell had been very ill.

"They tapped him!" she said excitedly, and a clerk near us looked up in alarm. "Dr. Ryan came and took a pint and a cup of fluid from him. He had pneumonia and pleurisy and infection. The doctor came every day when he was so bad. And his wife and Minnie and Annie nearly gave up on him." Here, she paused for breath.

"Who are Minnie and Annie?" I asked.

"They are his daughters. They stayed all the time he was so bad. I thought me'self he'd never get over it. When I turned down the lamp at night, he was a yellowish, greenish colour, an' he never ate a thing for two weeks."

"But he took liquids?"

"Yes, milk and eggnog and beef tea and all the medicine – morphine, strychnine and asafoetida. I was done out givin' the drinks and keeping on the fires. An' me heel got sore. The doctor said it was from me boot pressin' on me heel an' not takin' off me boots."

"But you feel all right now?"

"Well, I am afraid I have leakerage of the heart. I often feel a little dropping down," and she put her hand in the region of her stomach.

"But you wouldn't feel anything dropping down from your heart, Mrs. O'Brien, but anyway why don't you have an examination?"

"Yes, I will. I'll be givin' me house a bit of a cleanin'– then I'll go."

She had always looked and seemed to be in good health, her ruddy appearance and her energy seemed to decry any serious illness, but at different times, I had come upon Mrs. O'Brien, braced against a wall with her hand in the vicinity of her stomach, in the throes of what might be a mortal illness.

"Oh, Mrs. O'Brien, what is the matter!" I was at first

alarmed, then I became used to these attacks, as she seemed to always recover quickly. I thought it must be an attack of indigestion. She always gave the same explanation, "You know I have leakerage of the heart, Nurse." I thought of this now as she left the store. Perhaps there was something wrong with her heart.

I continued on my way out to my rooming house, passing through Queen's Square with its monument of soldiers in a perpetual state of going to war, with its fountain sending out its continuous showering of spray. Although it was a bright September day, there was a chill in the air that forecast another winter. Passing along the benches in front of the Confederation Building, the falling leaves danced around my head as they fluttered gracefully to the ground.

An Unusual "Undertaking"

Gillis and I had been in the same class during our training and had often worked together in the wards. As was the case with Helen Martin, Isabel Gillis was just Gillis to her friends. She was a good-looking girl with a soap-ad complexion and grey-blue eyes. I was off duty from a case at the hospital when Gillis invited some of the nurses out to her home at North River for supper and to spend the evening. Nobody refused the invitation because we all looked forward to enjoying the cheery comfortable Gillis home and their gracious hospitality.

At supper, we ate at a long table set with Limoges china and cut glass. The supper seemed a banquet to the nurses after the plain fare of the hospital. We hungrily helped ourselves to cold chicken, salad, tomatoes, biscuits, pie, cake, cookies, and strawberry jam served in small individual glass dishes.

Mrs. Gillis sat at the end of the table, her cheeks pink

from exertion, her eyes very blue. Widow of a civil servant of the federal government, she now had only her daughter and her daughter's friends to think about, and her demeanour was one of concern that everyone might not have all the food they wished.

After the table was cleared, Martin played the piano, and all care was forgotten as she pounded out Yankee Doodle Dandy, There's A Long, Long Trail A-Winding and other wartime favourites. Then we got out the Victrola, rolled up the fine broadloom rug, and danced for a while on the polished living room floor. I was picking up the waltz and foxtrot from Gillis and Martin who were very good dancers. Previously, I had been more used to the less complicated steps of the square dance common to the rural areas. Now I felt very modern and up-to-date. But alas, the party would be the last of its kind for many months to come.

When we were preparing to leave, it was mentioned that we might not be able to practice our dancing again until the Spanish flu epidemic was over. Gatherings were being discouraged. The Charlottetown Patriot had published a warning to that effect.

In parts of the country, the flu had reached epidemic proportions. Some cases had developed into pneumonia. I had lost one case in Charlottetown and I had heard of other deaths. People were becoming afraid of contracting the germs which brought life in the community virtually to a halt. There was little visiting and some schools were closed. Only those who had had the flu and had recovered were free of fear. Then they would recount the miseries that they had undergone, and invariably, how grateful they were to have survived.

And so, I was not surprised that my next call was to nurse a woman who had contracted the flu. My patient was an old lady whose lungs had been affected, and because of her age, she was not able to fight against it. After some sleepless nights and anxious days, the people of the house decided to call in Mrs. O'Brien to help me with the nursing and do whatever else was needed.

She appeared in the kitchen as a beneficent angel, very large in a raccoon coat, her head done up in a thick scarf, her frosted eyeglasses glittering in the light from the oil lamp as she removed high boots, the fur coat, and a sweater.

"It's the coldest weather in years. That's what *Dodd's Almanac* said. I got one," she announced. "We were a long time on the road, but as soon as I git thawed out here, I'll watch for a while, while you rest."

A baseburner in the hall was sending out cheerful heat day and night. Here in the parlour, I could rest on the red plush sofa, but I could sleep very little. There were enlarged pictures on the wall of sombre-eyed, dead relatives looking down at me from large, ornate frames. There was also a large marble clock in the shape of a tombstone that made a knell-like sound as it tolled out the hours of the night. I did not believe my patient would recover, and I tried unsuccessfully to overcome my depression.

The following day, I addressed a few remarks to the

Almighty in regard to my own demise if I should lose another patient. As I feared, my patient passed away. Pneumonia has been called the old person's friend and perhaps that was so because my patient did not appear to suffer. The family sent for the undertaker and soon a message came to me saying that he wanted to see me in the snow-filled garden. I had been used to well-dressed undertakers who operated with courage and despatch, but the unkempt man with long, black fingernails, whose clothes were dirty and unpressed, and who moved away from me as soon as I came near, was unlike any undertaker I had never seen!

"Don't come near," he said fearfully. "You see, I have no wife, so if I took the flu, I would have nobody to look after me. I am not going in that house!" He backed away, still looking frightened.

Other undertakers were called, but they were too busy because of so many deaths, unless the family could wait several days. They were willing to sell them a coffin and that was obtained very quickly. Then the family asked me to take charge of the laying out. I told Mrs. O'Brien that she would have to help me. "Glory be to God," she gasped and then produced a flask of whisky from her bag of "couterments" with which she fortified herself for the task ahead. I did not want to take a chance on imbibing since I had to remember the preparation of the dead that we were taught in the hospital. Mrs. O'Brien was also familiar with the simple rites, but we had difficulty with the eyes which would not close. Even pennies laid on the lids, a time-honoured procedure and endorsed by

Mrs. O'Brien, proved ineffective. I had heard someone say that she had always worn eyeglasses, and when I put them on her, I thought they improved her appearance.

Mrs. O'Brien looked down with disapproval. "Yes, but glory be, you can't put glasses on a corpse, Nurse. What could she see now?"

After some further effort, we got the eyes closed and looked down admiringly at our finished work when the coffin rested on chairs in the parlour. When friends and neighbours came to pay their respects, Mrs. O'Brien welcomed them in proudly. No doubt she felt we had done well and wanted to have our work seen and appreciated.

The pallbearers, the family, and others not ill with flu, accompanied the remains to the graveyard later in the day, where a short burial service was held by her minister.

Mrs. O'Brien and I were ready to leave, but we could not go until the following day when a train would pass through the district. Now we found that our separate couches were needed for relatives who had come from a distance for the funeral. When night came, I looked askance at the freshly made bed where our patient had so recently lain. But there was no help for it. We would have to sleep in that bed, for it was the only one available. Mrs. O'Brien at first objected strenuously, but I was too tired to care. After blessing herself several times, she got in beside me and soon I could hear her rhythmic snoring. The fatigue brought on by long nights of watching and tending the patient made us forget all else.

In the morning, we boarded the train and were headed

back to Charlottetown. As I listened to the hum of the wheels turning on the rails, I looked out the window at the grove of hardwood trees. The freshly fallen snow covered the branches and glinted on the fields beyond. The sight lifted my spirits. Even in the coldest of months, the beauty of the country brought me strength to start a new day.

When I Coughed,
Me Liver Flopped Over

That winter, the snow piled high on either side of the narrow sidewalks, and this did not bode well for travelling, should I get a country case.

It was cold outdoors but nice and warm inside. I had washed my hair, and because of its length, it took a long time to dry.

"Miss MacRae, you are wanted down here," a voice called from the landing. I rose quickly, wrapped a scarf around my head and hurried down to the front door. A big man in a curly, cloth coat was standing by the radiator. He was wrapped up with a green scarf done in the figure-eight style around his face and fur cap so that only his eyes and his nose, red and swollen from the cold, with an unwelcome drop at the end, were visible. There were drops in his eyes, too, but he wasn't crying and his eyebrows were covered with frost. He removed leather mitts, then thick, woollen gloves and held out big red hands to the warmth.

He had the detached air of a servant as he said, "The Myers are all sick with the flu and their doctor, Dr. Ryan, said you might come out and nurse them for a spell. They live at Kelly's Bridge, that is about eight miles out. I have a good horse and they sent an extra buffalo robe. They sent a brick too, for your feet. You can heat it here. They are good, kind people with a good farm. You'll be warm there and get plenty of grub."

"Yes, I suppose I could go," I replied. My hair was not yet dry, but I piled it high on my head and put on an extra scarf as protection against the cold. I put on my fur coat which I had bought with my first paycheque. It was impossible to take enough uniforms, a bathrobe, etc. in one suitcase, so two must be packed. It would seem alarming to the patient and to the relatives in the home to arrive with two since it might suggest a long illness and no little expense, but it couldn't be helped.

The sleigh was of a low, box type, painted red, with only a little of the paint worn off. There were warm robes, so we would not suffer from the cold. As we drove off, bells pealing merrily from the horse's harness, I thought of Dr. Ryan who was getting old now but who had never refused to go out if he was needed. With a true missionary spirit, through rain, hail, blinding snow or anything the elements could produce, he had gone. And how hard it was to travel, often over snow-filled unbroken roads, to the homes of the sick. That thought helped me to face the cold wind from the Gulf that bedevilled us as soon as we left the shelter of the city.

Finally, we left the pavement and took the secondary road. There was only one track and that, I guessed, had been made by my companion coming in. We moved slowly then with the horse throwing back his head and ploughing through drifts and across fences where a strand of wire showed through. Sometimes we drove through a farmer's yard, where curious people watched us from the kitchen window.

"Are you getting cold?" my companion asked, through lips thick with cold and a moustache heavily dropped down with icicles as his scarf had fallen down a bit. "Just about a mile to go."

Yes, I was getting cold, and I noticed that one fur-lined glove which I had worn over my woollen one was missing. My hand had been numb, and I hadn't noticed it falling off.

There was one bad stretch of road where the sleigh tipped and swayed dangerously in a series of deep hollows, called pitches, until at last it stood on its side, and I was tipped out with my suitcases following possessively after me.

The man looked at me with consternation. He was covered with snow himself, frost and icicles hung from his face and his scarf. He staggered towards me, leaving the horse down on the road in a tangle of harness and upset sleigh. "Did you get hurt?"

No, I wasn't hurt, but I thought I would finish the rest of the journey on foot, for the house was not far away. I tramped along in the snow on feet that were numb with the cold. I hoped the house would be warm.

Mrs. Myers met me at the door. She was a thin, pale woman with her hair done up in a blue scarf. She apologized for this as she took me inside. I found the farm house up-to-date with a furnace, electric lights and running water. Mrs. Myers was very tired and said she was afraid the house was untidy and her work neglected because they had been working night and day with the children.

It was good to get into the warm house. I took off my scarves and felt my hair. It was hard and stiff and I realized it was frozen.

"Warm yourself now, before you start working," Mrs. Myers said. The children were sick, but they were getting better. There were two little girls and a two-year-old boy who had the worst of it. And the mother was exhausted, having recently suffered an attack herself.

I found them all in the living room which had been converted into a hospital ward with Mrs. O'Brien in charge. But now that a trained nurse had come, she would spend part of the time in the kitchen with Mrs. Myers, for Mrs. O'Brien was versatile and could quickly change from one occupation to another. She took me around and introduced me to the patients. She went first to the crib of the youngest, a little solemn-faced boy who sucked continually. "This is little Jacob: weaned the wrong time of the moon," she said, looking compassionately at the child, then nodding wisely at me.

"And this is Gerty. A nice little girl, ain't you, dear? And this is Lillie Belle. She is three and Gerty is five. They is all nice children." But she told me later that they were "incorrible" and "Jacob keeps on moving the bed, jerkin' it like a cradle."

Mrs. Myers came in and gave the instructions about medicine and treatment. Every hour, there seemed to be some treatment or medicine, and Mrs. Myers was afraid something would be neglected.

"Did you give Lillie Belle her cough medicine?" she asked me.

"No, but I will in ten minutes. I thought it would be much simpler if they were all given at the same time."

"Well, the doctor said every three hours."

"Did you rub Gertrude's chest?"

"Yes, I just did that."

"Did you give Jacob his milk? And be careful in case he throws it up when he coughs."

"I am going to get it now."

"What is Lillie Belle's temperature? She looks flushed, did you take it?"

But to get her to leave the children at night was the hardest of all. The anxiety she felt for her children shook her confidence in the nursing profession. She tried to remember all she should tell me, but she was very tired, and she feared she might forget some of the many things that crowded her mind.

"You won't let the kitchen fire down, will you, because there will be a draft on Lillie Belle's feet if you do. I left the milk in the pantry and I brought in some ice for the night. You will have to watch little Jacob for if he cries, he gets blue in the face."

I tried to calm the overwrought mother as best I could, and soon we got her to go to her own bed, in which she had not rested for many nights.

Mrs. O'Brien came in at eleven to sit with me while I had tea. She had been nursing her brother's children who had the flu. "And glory be, Nurse the way we worked with the kids! Two of them was blue in the face for almost a week. We was poultcin' them an' we used a gallon of goose grease an' the doctor was comin', every day an' glory be, Nurse, we was all so done out when they started to get better that we coulda slept in our tracks and then" … a pause for breath… "didn't I come down with it m'self. I never suffered so much in my life. I was all covered with spots, pink, red and purple an' when I coughed, me liver, I think it was, flopped over like this." She illustrated with a small checked towel.

"I never would have got over it only I took Morton's Liver and Kidney pills. They're great. Me father took over one hundred boxes." After a brief pause, she looked over and said, "But your tea will be gettin' cold."

Mrs. O'Brien slept in a downstairs bedroom, and during the night as I worked and watched, I could hear her snoring loudly. Once she arose and stood at the door to ask how everything was going. Her hair was done up in tight curlers, and she wore a flowing white gown.

And Mrs. Myers came down once, groggy with sleep, but she soon went back to bed satisfied that all was well. The morning was coming and they had had a fair night. None of the children had awakened yet.

Then Jacob awoke and began to cough. The coughing

stopped suddenly and when I looked over to his bed it was hard to see in the dim light if he was blue. He was, decidedly. There was an anxious second, then a gasp, then lusty crying. "Nursie, make the bed stop moving," he sobbed. I went over to comfort him.

In a few days, my patients were almost well. However, they required many stories and much entertainment, and it was hard to get them settled down for the night, for they had spent so much of the day in bed that there was no bedtime. The next night, to quiet the children, I suggested that they say their prayers and the idea was welcomed by Gertrude. She knelt down at the side of her bed and asked all the blessings.

"Dear God, bless Mommy and Daddy, and Mrs. O'Brien and the nurse, and dear God, I'll not say, 'you dirty bastard' anymore." This was not all – the prayers must be said in different positions around the bed, but at last Gertrude's prayers were over.

Lillie Belle's were next, but she got through hers in a shorter time because she did not remember many of the words.

Only Jacob's remained to be said. He sat up in his bed, his teddy bear tossed aside, and listened intently as I began, "Now I lay me down to sleep...." I waited for him to repeat the line, but he had lately acquired the words, "Yes, sir" and "No, sir," and he thought this a good time to use them. "No, ter," he said, and "yes, ter" after each line.

Feeling the last prayer had been a failure, I went to the kitchen and sat down with a book, but I could hear the conversation in the living room which was still on a religious theme.

"Let's pretend that God is here in the room with us," said Gertrude, the leader.

"No, not here. Upstairs," said Lillie Belle.

"Yes. He is here and He is going to sleep with me."

"No! Goin' to sleep wif me," Lillie Belle insisted.

"All right, then. God can sleep with you and Jesus can sleep with me." She was learning to give in to her younger sister. But she was also getting very sleepy and soon all was quiet.

In the morning, I carried the breakfast trays out to the pantry and was cleaning them off when I heard a scream from the living room. I hurried in and saw that it was Jacob who had screamed. Gertrude was standing by his bed with a bottle of ink in one hand and a spoon in the other, giving a very good imitation of Mrs. O'Brien "Glory be!" she said. "Will you take this or do I have to force ya?"

"Gory be! Take dis or force ya," said the copycat.

I snatched the ink, thankful that I had stopped the stunt at the beginning. I saw that I must watch them every minute until Mrs. O'Brien would relieve me at noon. They were getting just well enough to be really frisky.

Mr. Myers had the same impersonal way I had noticed in his hired man. They came in for their meals, said little, looked at the newspapers, then went out to the barn to feed and water the stock, or to clean out the buildings. It was a well-kept place, and because of the deep snow, Hungarian partridges and other wild birds mingled with the barn pigeons in the barnyard looking for grain.

One afternoon, I ventured out, having strapped on a pair of snowshoes that were kept on the back porch. I tramped a bit through the woods behind the barns, noticing the numerous tracks that told of rabbits. I wondered, if I were to marry a farmer, would I be happy in this kind of existence? I had been too busy fighting the battle on the home front against the Spanish Influenza to have met any interesting matrimonial prospects. All social occasions had been cut out for fear of spreading the dreaded germs. The important thing now was to go on from day to day.

One day, when I was preparing a diet in the pantry off the kitchen, Mr. Myers came in, partially closed the door and lost the impersonal manner. He stood there sombre-eyed in his overalls and heavy, checked shirt and said, "How much are you going to charge me, Nurse?"

This was unexpected, and I thought, unnecessary. They were not poor, for they had both a car and a truck, while many farmers managed with only a truck, sometimes only a car. The house had all the conveniences, except perhaps a Frigidaire, and Mrs. Myers spoke of getting that.

"Well, nurses get five dollars a day," I said, thinking he would consider that exorbitant. After all, he would think she is only a young girl, why should she get such high wages?

In fact, hearing of the wages did seem to be a shock. He reached for a glass of water as if to steady himself. "You see, Nurse, it is pretty hard on the pocketbook to pay wages to two nurses. You understand," he said gloomily.

I wondered if the children were well enough for me to leave. I mentioned this to Mrs. O'Brien, "Glory be, Nurse, don't think of goin' yet!" she exclaimed. "Don't go until all them coughs is better an' Mrs. Myers is feelin' stronger. An' here is a bit of campfire to put in your pocket so's you won't take it. I always carry some with me."

"Thanks." I sniffed appreciatively at the camphor. I liked the smell even if my faith in its germicidal action was negligible.

A few days later when the children were moved back to their own rooms, I knew I wasn't needed and I prepared to leave. Mr. Myers came forward and paid uncomplainingly, and Mrs. Myers told me how glad she had been to have my help with the children.

As I hurried to catch the train, which did not stop long at this siding, I realised I would not have enough time to check my suitcases. I would have to bundle them into the passenger car with me.

"Here is a girl coming with two big bags!" a man said. "Good Lord, make way for her!"

Strong arms lifted my suitcases onto the racks at the end of the car, and as I turned to take the nearest empty seat, I saw the reflection of myself in the mirror above the seat. I thought that the dark circles under my eyes made me look like one of the winged monkeys in *The Wizard of Oz* that I had been reading to the children during their convalescence. I had also lost weight, and considering everything, I decided to rest at home for a few days.

Try the Goose Grease

When I arrived home, I found my family all recovering from the flu which seemed to be everywhere and was keeping the community in a state of anxiety. There was an epidemic of whooping cough, too, and a few cases of pneumonia.

One evening, the hired man from a neighbour's house came for me. He was a more articulate type than the Myers' hired man, and he brought us all up to date on the situation without waiting for questioning. He was on very familiar terms with his employer, evidently.

"The baby has the whooping cough and it takes blue spells," he said. "Molly and Wess was up all last night and Wess ain't very well after having the flu. They got Mrs. O'Brien to come from the Myers and she is poulticin' all the time. They sent for the doctor to come out today, but he was away." He dropped into a chair and continued, after cutting off a plug of tobacco with a pen knife, "Mrs.

O'Brien doesn't think the baby will get better. She says it's not the time of the moon to get over a bad attack of whooping cough." He took a bite of tobacco and shook his head. "Molly wants to know if you can come for a day or two, and if youse got any goose grease will you bring it with you. There's no knowin' when the doctor will get back out here. There's so many sick."

I dressed hastily. We would cross a field for it would be much shorter than going by road. We had only gone a short distance away from the woods when a great stretch of ice glittered in the moonlight before us. I was wearing a hat with a feather that was supposed to fall gracefully down the side but which now waved grotesquely in the gusts of wind that met us on the open field. We wavered uncertainly on the ice, and I clung to his mittened hand to stay upright.

Soon the house of Molly and Wess Bone came into view. It was snow-covered and gleamed white in the moonlight, and as it was set about with many coniferous trees, it reminded me of an exquisite Christmas card. Now, because of sickness, light gleamed in every window.

When we reached the house and opened the kitchen door, we were met by a gust of warm, close air. It was filled with various odours such as onions, vinegar, and drugs that were used in the treatment of the disease. We were standing by the fire when the child's mother came in. She was flushed and nervous. "Will you come up and see the baby, Miss MacRae? Perhaps you would know what they do in the hospital if they get blue when they cough. We have been so worried and upset."

The house was smaller and not as grandly furnished as the Myers', but it was cozy, with a wood heater warming the upstairs hall.

In the sickroom, Mrs. O'Brien had taken charge. The doctor had left a prescription and oil for rubbing, but in the urgency and anxiety of the moment when the baby's life seemed to be in danger, Mrs. O'Brien had turned to a remedy that she believed never failed. It was goose grease.

"Just give a spoon or two of that and it'll be all right. I tried it on me sister's children," she said.

But I was doubtful. The doctor hadn't ordered it, and it might make the baby worse. I looked anxiously at the infant, then hurried to heat some camphorated oil.

Just then the baby's father came into the room. He was still suffering from the flu but was allowed out of bed.

As he stood looking down at the suffering baby, it started coughing again, and Mrs. O'Brien rushed over. It was turning blue and she became greatly alarmed.

"Glory be to God, Nurse, you'll have to try the goose grease! Just try it," she said, bringing over a spoon and a bottle.

I looked doubtfully at the father who was standing with his back to the light. He was pale and looked anemic. "Yes, that seems to be the cure, so they all say," he said.

But I was uncertain. What if the child should die? Would the parents feel it was my fault because I had refused to try a remedy that they felt might help it? I supposed everybody in the neighbourhood believed in goose grease.

"Well, if you want to give it yourself…" I hesitated when a hush fell on the house. It was a hush that I was to notice many times. "The doctor is here," I heard somebody say.

Here was a higher authority and even Mrs. O'Brien was cowed and said nothing more about the goose grease. It was pleasant to think that it was now the doctor's responsibility.

Dr. Ryan came in, big enough, but the blustering manner had gone. I thought he seemed very tired. He looked at the baby and suggested giving a serum, and thought perhaps steam from a croup tent might help. His eyes were heavy-lidded and half-closed.

Mr. Bone said "You're very tired, Doctor. Would you like to lie down?"

"Yes," Dr. Ryan said. "I was up all last night on a case and the night before I was called out towards morning. I believe I'll just lie down until morning. I could sleep there," he said, pointing to a small bedroom off the larger room. "Or is that your bed, Wess? I don't want to take your bed."

"That's all right, Doc, I can sleep at the side. I am not very big. Sure, lie down there." The doctor was so overcome with fatigue that he did not argue any further.

The door of the bedroom was kept open to let heat from the stove in the hall enter, and thus it was impossible not to see the sleeping arrangements. The doctor removed his coat and shoes, and in red-toed wool socks, he went to look again at the baby.

"Yes, let it have some moist air. Steam from a kettle will have to do. Keep your kettle boiling on the hall stove there."

Having given this order, he threw himself down and the bedclothes made a great mound over his round, pink face. Soon the rhythmical sound of snoring was heard.

Though it was not unusual for people to sleep two or three in a bed, the doctor had come to the house so exhausted that he fell into a deep sleep, and unknowingly, was taking up three-quarters of the bed space. Wess was unable to get any sleep. Finding it impossible to keep from rolling off his side of the bed, he came out fully dressed and shook his head. "It's no use trying to sleep. I think I'll go downstairs and make tea. A cup of tea will do us all good." He left and soon I heard him calling that the tea was ready.

"You go down, Miss MacRae," Mrs. O'Brien said. "I ain't hungry now."

I came down to the dining room where Wess was presiding over the teacups. It seemed odd to be taking tea at one o'clock in the morning with a neighbour with whom I'd barely been acquainted previously. Then I went back to relieve Mrs. O'Brien, who was probably very tired, having been on the case for over a week.

Morning was coming when the doctor left the house, and the child did seem a little better. Because there was some improvement, I felt that it was all right to leave. Before I left, Mrs. O'Brien gave me an interesting account of how she had managed and what had been expected of her in the way of nursing.

"Glory be, Nurse, I cut up a hundred pounds of onions this winter for poultices. But they saved Mrs. McCarty's life. We pulled her through with them," she declared.

Just then, Molly fluttered in with some dollar bills in her hand. "You must take something for your night's work, Elizabeth," she said.

"Oh, it's not worthwhile, not for just one night," I said, thinking that they were neighbours, and in a farming community, each member helped the others in times of stress and sickness.

"Well, did you fellas have any punkins last year? I had a lot. Would you take a bottle of punkin jam? It is very good."

"Yes. I don't know whether Aunt Mary has any or not. It does look good," I said, looking from the jam to Molly's white, tired face.

"And we have a lot of these salt mackerel. Would you take one? They are nice for a change."

With a wave of my hand to Molly and Mrs. O'Brien at the door, and rather laden down with the jam and mackerel, I made my uncertain way across the icy field. It was the latter part of February and I faced a wind that caught my hat and took it sailing across the field. Retrieving my hat, I followed a sheltered lane to the back of our house and arrived home with the fruits of my night's labour intact.

Soon I found solace in uninterrupted sleep in my cozy room in the old farmhouse, with only the chiming grandfather's clock in the front hall to disturb my dreams.

The "Demon Rum"

Back in my room at Brighton, I looked out over a frozen Government Pond. Some children were playing and skating, happily enjoying the winter. In this warm room, winter did not seem too severe. I reasoned that by the law of averages, my next case would probably be in Charlottetown where nursing would be undeniably easier, in heated rooms. In the country, I had often been obliged to change into an icy uniform in a frigid temperature. There, I had coal or wood fires to keep on, but in Charlottetown, there were bathrooms with running water, and what was important too, one could easily make contact with friends.

But one evening, Dr. Burke telephoned asking if I would go out to the country on another maternity case. He would call for me. He had a horse and sleigh, and we would drive out together.

The temperature was sub-zero when I climbed into the sleigh beside Dr. Burke. A round face was only slightly showing above a turned-up fur collar of his coat, and little showing below his large fur cap.

"I hope you're warmly dressed, Miss MacRae," he said with some concern. "We have about three miles to drive." The sleigh bells rang comfortingly, but there was a bitter wind off the Gulf to the northeast.

Yes, I was all right in regard to clothing, but along with odours of drugs that often cling to doctor's clothing, there was something else. An odour of whiskey was on his breath. Well, I couldn't blame him for taking a drink when starting on this cold drive, and I wondered if a drink in my own case might not have been a good thing. But no, I was afraid. The "Demon Rum," I had heard that so many times. One might get the drinking habit, and then the words "she drinks" would be heard, designating the lowest in human degradation.

Dr. Burke was cheerful and even told a story – "You know, there was an old lady in the ward. She always seemed unhappy and one day when I was making my rounds, I found her crying. I found out what was the matter. She wanted to smoke but felt she was forbidden. She took a pipe out of her bosom where she had it concealed and said, 'Here, doctor you may as well take this. It's no good to me here.' I told her to smoke if she wanted to. She could smoke in the utility room if she wished. So now she is happy. She rocks and smokes."

I was too cold for conversation, and despite being dressed warmly, I shivered. It was hard to judge Dr. Burke too severely for imbibing in the "Demon Rum," as he had many trips like this one on a winter night.

Before very long, we arrived at the farmhouse. We ducked the icicle hanging from the door and entered.

The patient's mother was in charge, a small, thin woman with a slightly anxious expression. I had often noticed this expression in the faces of Maritimers, perhaps because they had to work so hard to make a comfortable living. Perhaps because they had faced, too many times, the cruel winds that swept over the dashing waves and the snow-filled fields.

"She is not far advanced in labour," Dr. Burke said a bit later as he came to the kitchen. "I think I may well go back to town and come out again in the morning. She will last to the morning all right," he said to me, looking at me as if asking my permission to go. "You have the telephone to call me if you need me, all right?" He began putting on his coat.

Usually, the patient dreaded the doctor's leaving. There was a loss of security. It was good to have the doctor right there, but my patient seemed resigned. Perhaps the presence of a nurse helped. Only her mother looked a bit more anxious as the doctor left.

I prepared for the case, and when the patient went off to sleep, I decided to lie down in the adjoining room. She would call me if needed. She did call a few hours later. Her pains had started again.

I called the doctor, and perhaps he had been expecting my call, for he seemed to be about ready to start the journey again. He said, "Yes, I'll come at once." Later I was glad to hear the sound of the horse and sleigh in the yard, but when Dr. Burke came in, I saw at once that all was not well. He had been seeking additional comfort from the bottle in preparation for the second cold drive. He swayed slightly, his face had a dull, stupid look, and he glanced at me without interest. After a quick look at the patient, he said, "I think I'll lie down for a bit, nursh," as if that was a most reasonable thing to do.

My patient's mother looked at the door, and her anxious expression deepened. "Oh, my, my," she said under her breath. Soon I heard sounds of snoring from the couch in the living room. Dr. Burke was asleep. Perhaps he might rouse himself in this emergency. But if not, I must depend on my patient's mother for help. I did not feel so inadequate as I had at Joe Morgan's. Perhaps my spells of nursing had strengthened me. I prepared myself as well as possible and told my patient's mother what she was supposed to do. We made ties for cord out of cotton, twisted thread. Although she kept repeating, "Oh, my, my," she did as I asked her. A woman who had lived on a farm and had borne five children, and who had worked out in the fields as well as in the house, was ready for anything unusual.

"I'll go and get a big apron," she said.

The case was coming on quickly. Perhaps I could rouse Dr. Burke. I went over to the sofa and tugged, not too gently, at his shoulder.

"Wake up, Dr. Burke, wake up! Your patient needs you now. Come, come!"

"Wash that, nursh?" he said thickly.

"Get up, Dr. Burke."

"Wash you want?"

"Get up, Dr. Burke!"

"Trouble with you, Miss MacRae, is that you're too fushy." Then angrily, "You're fushing at me now, MacRae. You should leave me alone."

"But your patient needs you, Dr. Burke."

"Never desert a friend in need, I always say. I said that all through McGill. What dosh she want?"

"You are on a maternity case. Come and help if you are coming. Come now!"

He sat up for a minute as if he were trying to think. Then his head fell forward, a lock of his hair fell over his face, and he sank down again. It was of no use to rouse him.

"I can't get him awake, not enough to take charge," I said to my patient's mother.

"Oh, my! my!" she said in distress as a great flood of water poured onto the bed. "The bag of waters, the bag of waters has burst. What will you do, Nurse?" She was distressed but reasonably calm.

"Hand me some of those sterilized dressings."

"Yes, Nurse."

"And minutes later, "Hand me the cord, ties, and scissors."

"Yes, Nurse."

And there was the baby. It had been slapped and was breathing. When I looked up minutes later, I saw the expression of the grandmother's face had changed from anxiety to happiness. She was no longer distressed, and she knew what to do with the stained linen and a bundle wrapped in newspaper oozing blood. She had a granddaughter. "I am glad she is a girl. You can dress them so cute. My daughter has her clothes ready, Nurse. I'll get them. Her last two were boys." She hurried away, then came back later to help me make the patient comfortable.

"Where is the doctor now, Nurse?" My patient asked, more out of curiosity than of need.

"He is asleep on the couch in the living room, but now that it is morning, I imagine he will waken."

I would tell the doctor now that all was over. I would make an announcement completely in reverse. He was waking a bit and looked bewildered when I said, "She has a lovely girl, Doctor." He looked at me without surprise. He blinked, yawned and rose from the couch. He prepared to go but first checked the patient. "I'll see her tomorrow, Nurse," he said. No doubt he was ashamed, and when my patient's husband paid him at the door, I knew the fee would not be too high. He could only charge for prenatal care. As he put on his scarf, he said to me, "This travelling at night is too hard. I am thinking of only doing hospital work. Who wants the likes of this in the winter?"

It was disillusioning to see someone as skilled in his profession go this far in neglecting his duties. Thinking that I could handle the situation was not a sufficient excuse. I could not help comparing him with Dr. Grant. He would never have let me or the patient down in such a way. He was always ready to accept any challenges and meet them head on.

But when my thoughts turned to Dr. Grant, I would often wonder if the two of us could make a good match. I recognized the extra attention he paid to me. Despite his gruff exterior, I couldn't deny that he was a caring man, committed to his profession. But would he be as committed to a family? The main problem with Donald Grant was that I always felt that I could never come up to his high standards. Mine was the quieter way. With country nursing, I had become more dependent on my solitary walks, on sketching, and my quiet reading times. Would full-time life in the city be tolerable? I put the thought out of my head.

Once I saw both baby and mother were doing well, I prepared to leave. Perhaps it was the unsettling thoughts of a life in the city, but I longed for the quiet of home. I would take my name off the registry tomorrow and be secure in the knowledge that my break would be uninterrupted.

Mrs. O'Brien Proves Her Worth

My friends in Charlottetown deplored so much country nursing. In the country, one could have little social life in terms of entertainment, dances, movies, etc. Then, darkly, the thought occurred to me that I would never marry unless I settled in one place long enough to meet someone. "Get cases in town and have some fun," advised a nurse who was going steady. For me, continual watching at a bedside with hypos given every four hours was a discouraging factor in any budding relationship.

Sometimes we were completely snowbound. Then when the storm was over, links with the outside world were taken up again: the mailman passing, the smoke of the neighbour's chimney, and the call to inquire about the sick.

Bound together by the fear of death, anxiety, and long hours of watching, the nurse became one of the family unit. There was Sunday church-going, where in the Protestant church, the minister prayed for the sick and those who waited upon them, and in the Catholic church, sad, sweet music played, suggesting the shortness of this life and the nearness of eternity.

But when the threat of severe winter storms was past, Martin would sometimes invite me to her home near Bedeque for a few days if we could arrange to be off together. The St. Patrick's concert in that area was a greatly anticipated event in the communities for miles around. We would go with Martin's brothers, Bill and George, and sometimes others from the neighbourhood. Later we would gather at the Martin home to talk over the gala evening.

It was a time of great conviviality. The fast-disappearing snow, the running water, the calling of birds, the pussy willows bursting above the snow – all seemed to suggest happiness. If there was still snow on the ground, everybody went to the concert in a big bobsleigh. There might be deep pitches in places where sleighs had cut valleys in the road. When the sleigh lurched to one side, someone would grab your arm to keep you from falling out. It was all very companionable – an adventure that made the quick rhythm of the jigs and reels in the hall more enjoyable.

The highlight of the St. Patrick's concert was the Irish play, and the audience would be most delighted if there was an Irish washerwoman type of character in it, with a brogue so thick you could cut it with a knife. And of course, the contrasting English gentry would be portrayed to the best of their ability, with gesturing and dropping of the "r's". After the performance, you might hear, "Didn't

Bobby Murnaghan do the English Lord to perfection?" These dramatic efforts were often the links that fused the community together, whatever their politics or religion.

Besides enjoying the easy-going gaiety of these visits with the Martins, I found that Bill Martin and I shared a deep mutual interest in reading. When his work at grading potatoes for the warehouse was slack, he would sometimes return to the house and we would talk interminably about many topics. My reading, heretofore, had been mostly in novels, for escape from the routine of nursing, or in medical journals. But following my discussions with Bill in the late afternoons, lingering over cups of tea, I discovered that I was becoming more interested in biographies and history rather than merely novels with an historical approach to life. I couldn't help comparing his approach to life with that of Donald Grant. Bill had developed a philosophy from observing people and events around him, and he was able to apply that philosophy to give meaning to his daily pursuits. Dr. Grant, on the other hand, was headed for success in his profession, and the people around him would be forced into the maelstrom of activity that would surround him. To him, the challenge was all. It was a prospect that I was not sure I could face.

While visiting at the Martin home, I was called to nurse a Mr. Frank Carpenter who was threatened with pneumonia. Other members of the family were sick with flu. The Carpenter home was comfortable with some modern conveniences. Bathrooms and electricity were beginning to come to the country homes, and the Carpenters had been among the first to modernize their century-old farmhouse.

Dr. Ryan came soon after I arrived and explained that Mr. Carpenter must stay in bed and was on no account to get out as he wished to do. He was a thin, serious looking man who seemed a bit downhearted at the doctor's orders. Mrs. Carpenter and her four year old child were still confined to bed in the adjoining room. The child kept repeating, "I don't feel good," as she looked up through untidy hair. Mrs. Carpenter was a fair, pretty woman who was determined to be cheerful and make the best of things. She still had some temperature but was getting better and would soon be up. Their hired man had obtained a job in Halifax and had left them hastily. There were animals to be fed and watered. Mrs. Carpenter asked me if l thought Mrs. O'Brien would come. If she came to help in the house, it wouldn't be too hard for us to give the chickens and the yearling calves a bite each day, and there was a pump in the barn for water. The calf was still on the cow, and we could get a neighbour's boy to come in after school to clean the stables. Mrs. O'Brien seemed to be the solution. I was to call her to see if she could help.

Mrs. O'Brien agreed to come out right away, and as I waited for her to arrive, I busied myself making a pneumonia jacket that Dr. Ryan had ordered for Mr. Carpenter. These jackets were made of cotton-batting material, normally used to make quilts and comforters. They were made to cover the chest and back and were to ensure against chill. But they were always bulky and never did fit. I cut out the jacket in what I thought would be the right size, basted it up, then tried it on myself over my uniform. As I stood before the mirror in Mr. Carpenter's room, he watched me with great interest. He had heard the doctor's orders, but he thought the jacket was unnecessary. "That's right, Nurse, you may as well wear the jacket yourself. You'll need it more than I will if you are going to work out in the barn." He eventually consented to the idea and allowed the pneumonia jacket to be fitted on him.

When Mrs. O'Brien arrived, she was dressed for hard labour. She did not mind the idea of working in the barn. It was all in a day's work to her. She said, "Now, how'll we divide the work? If I pump the water, will you put down the hay?"

We entered the stable, warmed by the heat of the animals' bodies. They looked at us beseechingly with their dark eyes. Was the nurse's privilege of giving help and comfort for humans only? They were hungry. I climbed the ladder leading to the loft. Up there, I found a hayfork and started lifting up forkfuls from the hard-trampled piles of hay. Although I had lived on a farm, the work I had done in the fields and barn was very little. My father and brother had done all the chores and field work while I helped Aunt Mary or read a book. I continued tugging and throwing down the hay, and after what seemed to me a great deal of work, I asked Mrs. O'Brien if I had put down enough. "Glory be, Nurse, that ain't near enough!" So I continued. I paused for breath and looked out of a small window. I thought if one was a philosopher or wanted to find the meaning of life or a remedy for all the human ills, it would be just as possible to do so from a high barn window as sitting under a bow tree or up on a mountain. Here was seclusion and peace.

At last, the animals were fed and watered, but Mrs. O'Brien decided to take on another project. She wanted to move the calf away from the cow. "No need for the calf getting all the milk. We can let him get plenty, even if we milk a bit first. They all need milk in there and canned milk is terrible in your tea. Mr. Carpenter said I could move the calf to another stall."

She began by pulling, but the calf was stubborn. Why should he leave that warm body with the ever-flowing sustenance? After we had both tried pulling and shoving for some minutes, Mrs. O'Brien fell apart emotionally and cried, "Holy Mary, I'll kill you!" The extra spurt of energy seemed to do the trick, and we pushed him into the other stall.

Later in the afternoon, Mrs. O'Brien continued proving her worth. She came in with a plucked chicken in her hands, a few feathers clinging to her hair and dress, and a look of satisfaction on her face. "It'll make good soup for them that's sick and something to eat for ourselves."

Aunt Mary had been right about Mrs. O'Brien. She could do much necessary work and was invaluable in times of sickness!

In the evening, when the patients had been made comfortable and I had left Mr. Carpenter reading a new book by J.B. Priestly, I sat in the kitchen with Mrs. O'Brien who disapproved of the reading. "All the books he has there. He used to teach school they say, but I don't think farmin' and readin' go together, not too much."

"Have you ever read a book?" I asked Mrs. O'Brien.

"Yes, I did. I read one once." And Mrs. O'Brien's eyes became dreamy as she began a resume of her story. "It appears there was a woman who was trapped for days upon a mountain. She fell and was caught between rocks up there. There wasn't no way she could get out, and there was nothin' for her to eat. But a man heard her call. It appears he had a house not too far away, so he got her out and took her home to his house and fed her and nursed her back to life. It appears she was a rich woman and he wasn't too poor himself. Anyway, they fell in love and were married and were happy always." As Mrs. O'Brien told her story, her face took on a faraway, happy expression. For a few minutes, she, who had been deserted, was living vicariously through the life of a woman who had been tenderly nursed back to life and loved. She sighed then asked me if I had ever read *"Annie of the Gables."*

"Anne of Green Gables, yes, I've read most of L. M. Montgomery's books."

Mrs. O'Brien continued talking, "My Patrick liked to read. He liked them blood and thunder magazines, Westerns they call them. He had a set of books too. Fennimore Coopers, I think they was. A man had the books, but he was movin' away so he gave them to Patrick, not knowin' what to do with them. And sometimes when all me work was done, he would read to me about them people that was wanderin' in the woods. It was kinda interestin'. He liked to read, but he didn't go crazy about readin' like." She nodded towards Mr. Carpenter's door.

"What happened to your little girl, Mrs. O'Brien?" I asked and then regretted bringing back an old grief. She had told me of a child.

"I don't know exactly what happened. She took a high fever. We took her to the hospital and the doctor said she had some kind of tuberculosis. An awful quick kind. They called it galloping tuberculosis. There is nothing left of little Teresa now but the little white tombstone that I bought. It's awful pretty. Two little angels flying with a wreath of flowers carved on it and ribbons floating around all carved in the white marble."

I must change the subject, "Have you had many cases lately, Mrs. O'Brien?"

"Glory be, I am sick of bein' called out at night on baby cases. It's always the same, 'Hurry, Mrs. O'Brien. Come at once' or 'I'll call for you in five minutes!' or 'How soon can you get here, Mrs. O'Brien?' I had one case just goin' down by the day to keep an old couple. They was awful old. She used to go around with two canes and bent over. He was a bit smarter and used to do the washin' but not very good. Well, I cleaned and washed and cooked for them. They was pleased. At last she took a stroke and they both went into the infirmary. He paid me and gave me some things out of their house — a set of them views where you see double and a family album. It was his wife's album with her pictures in it, pictures with nice verses under them like, "Born on earth to bloom in Heaven." It was a picture of an old man with big whiskers. "He bloomed on earth" could have been under that one, if you ask me."

After a couple of days of looking after the animals as well as the patients, we had a visit from Bill Martin who came to see if we needed anything. Yes, we needed a pair of strong arms to move the hay! On the previous day, I had nearly fallen backwards through the hole in the centre of the loft because of my feeble efforts to dislodge the trampled hay. Bill laughed at my story and went out to the barn forthwith and put down enough hay to the centre floor of the barn to keep the animals chewing for three days.

After a few days of this routine, Mrs. Carpenter's temperature was normal and she was able to get out of bed. The child, Marilyn, and her father were progressing well. Marilyn was now playing with her dolls in bed, and Mr. Carpenter was able to read. He had a book of poems which he seemed to like very much. He looked up and said, "Have you ever read Omar Khayyam, Nurse?"

"Yes, when my friend, another nurse, and I were out camping last summer we had the book. He said, 'A Jug of Wine, A Loaf of Bread – and Thou,' but since we had no wine, we had to content ourselves with ginger ale!"

Mr. Carpenter laughed. "Yes," he said, "but I have heard that when Omar spoke of wine, he meant the wine of life." Then my patient sat up with his pneumonia jacket showing bulkily through his pajamas, and began to recite in a dramatic manner. "A book of verses underneath a bough..."

Mrs. Carpenter smiled and said, "I believe Frank is

better. It looks as if we are pretty well over the flu. When Frank begins to recite poetry, I know all is well. Sometimes when he is out in the barn, I hear him singing to the cows. I hope they like it."

They were happy, and the depressed spirits which often accompanied the flu had gone. It was an unusually cold day for March, but outside looked very bright, matching the mood in the home. It was almost as if we had been travelling in a tunnel and then suddenly came to the light.

Dr. Ryan came that afternoon and said that Mr. Carpenter was well enough that I could leave and that he needed me on another case. "I have a patient who has to have an appendix operation. She is pretty sick and I am afraid to move her over the rough roads. It is not going to be easy. I think the best way will be to get the men to get together some boards, a door would do, then put a small mattress on that, and let the men carry her to the station that way." He looked at me inquiringly, keen blue eyes in a weather-beaten face as he asked, "Could you come with me to help?"

Yes, I could go. I said goodbye to the Carpenters and climbed in the sleigh beside the fur-coated, warmly dressed doctor, his grey hair showing below a large fur cap. With hands encased in large, fur-lined driving mitts, he grasped the reins and urged the horse on.

For Medicinal Purposes Only

"Nursing in the country is hard," Dr. Ryan said as we drove along the country road. "It is hard to keep a uniform heat in the rooms."

I did not hear very well. My head was tied up with a thick scarf. I thought he said, "Keep uniforms neat."

"Yes, indeed," I agreed. "One needs a clean apron or uniform every day and that's hard especially if there is coal dust."

"What are you talking about, Nurse?" He looked at me with curiosity.

"I must have misunderstood you," and we both smiled at my mistake. It was hard to keep the rooms at a uniform temperature, too true. The fire would either be up or down, and if the wood burned completely out, one faced the very guilty feeling of having failed the patient.

When I entered the sick room, my patient was lying in her bed, almost apathetic. She stared into space without interest. She was completely at the mercy of others, whether for good or evil. She had been drugged for pain. I found some warm clothing but mostly she would be wrapped in blankets. But if she should take a weak turn on our way to the station, what could I do? The men came in to carry the stretcher across the fields to the railway station. The mother hovered over the preparations, seemingly helpless. As I put on my heavy coat, she came to me with a half-bottle of whiskey and put it in my pocket. "Just in case you might need it," she whispered. "We always keep some on hand for medicinal purposes."

Then she came to the door to see us off, her anxious figure framed by the doorway. There was a doubt that she would see her daughter alive again, but one never gave up hope. The sun came out bright and strong for March and the snow gave off thousands of reflective scintillating lights. A chick-a-dee chirped.

"She will be all right. You'll have her back soon, well and strong," I said to the mother.

The men were taking quick, even, purposeful steps, and it was hard for me, with my short legs, to keep up. I hurried along with the bottle of whiskey in my coat pocket, making me appear a bit lop-sided. A spring snow-fall followed by rain and ice meant that a hard crust of snow covered the fields. I found I could walk on top, but I still had trouble keeping up with the men who plunged through the crust at every step.

At the station, there was the difficulty of getting her on the train, but the men in charge seemed capable. My patient's brother came with us and was giving directions. An ambulance would meet the train in Charlottetown. What had seemed so very awkward in the beginning, worked out simply and well.

I left my patient in a hospital bed with nurses in their blue and white, the uniforms of nurses in training. I handed over the bottle of whiskey to the brother to be returned to their home in case it really was meant "for medicinal purposes only."

What's To Become of Ida May?

Home for the weekend, I was curled up on the sofa with a book when Uly came in. "When I was working out in the far field, Leoda called out to me that she was sick and she asked if I thought you would mind going to take her temperature," he asked. "She feels awful, worse in the afternoons. So I told her you would go." He looked at me expectantly.

I did not know Leoda very well, for I was what they called a "speaking acquaintance." I had never been to her home, but I sometimes met her in the store or on the country roads. I said I would go and asked Uly to come too, for Leoda might be out of firewood.

A short time later, Uly and I made our way across the farmlands towards Leoda's home. The roads had broken up and this would be the best way to travel if we could sidestep the muddy and watery places in the field. The March sun was warm and was melting the snow except in sheltered spots and in the woods.

Leoda Mooney had been married to an elusive Barney MacCourt who was always disappearing. But even this disappearing act had been, in a way, a satisfaction and a source of pride. He usually dressed in flashy, modern raiment, so different from the prosaically-clothed farmers and tradesmen. He had vanished the last time they were at the Provincial Exhibition, and Leoda had gone among the crowd of spectators asking for information, without success, and saying, "If you see anyone wearing a big white hat and tan raincoat and carrying an umbrella, that's him."

Leoda sold beer which was against the law, and since Barney had disappeared again, she had been brewing more because she depended on it for her living. I was thinking of this as we came to Leoda's small, unpainted home.

The yard was very untidy with old boxes, empty bottles and cans, and discarded odds and ends. The kitchen windowsills were filled with tomato cans, some containing tomato plants to be set out later in the season and some with geraniums and other flowers.

I knocked and heard Leoda's shrill voice call out, "Come in, I saw you comin'. No need to knock when you come to my house."

She had been sitting in an old rocking chair, but she rose when we entered, and I saw at once that she was indeed quite ill. Looking at her closely, I saw a tall, thin woman probably in her late twenties, in a faded dress and shawl around her shoulders. I thought the flushed cheeks, too bright eyes and shallow cough told a story. "How long have you been feeling sick?" I asked.

"Well, I haven't been real well for a year, I guess. I had the flu awful bad once, and I don't believe I ever got over it. I got a bottle of Father John's medicine an' I took Labrador Tea, and Life of Man, too. I used to go to the woods to get labrador and stew it. They're awful good, but I coughed and coughed until I thought I'd die! I haven't felt well enough to look after Ida May, poor kid," she added, looking over at her little girl who was three or four years old.

Ida May was washing her face in a basin of water that had been placed on a chair for her convenience. Although her hair hung in straggling locks about her face, and she was undoubtedly suffering from malnutrition, she was cute and attractive. I saw a strand of red yarn tied around each spindly leg, and since they were not garters, I wondered about it.

"What is that, Leoda?" I asked.

Oh, that's because she has growin' pains so bad in her legs. At first, I used to wrap red flannel around them, but now I just keep one ply of yarn there and she never has a pain," Leoda answered.

Uly came in and watched while Leoda's temperature was taken. As I waited for the thermometer to register, I noticed some details of the miserable, untidy room. The table was filled with unwashed dishes and empty cans, the floor was littered and unswept, but something unusual stood out: an axe stood by the doorway and part of the doorframe had been cut away. When I looked at the thermometer, I saw Leda's temperature was 102 degrees.

But she wanted to tell me about the door. I suppose she had noticed my interest.

"I had to cut that for firewood," she said. "We was so cold and you know we had bad storms this winter. There's some big blocks in the yard, but I can't split them." When Uly heard that Leoda was actually cutting away her house for firewood, he went out and split the blocks. Then Leoda began to talk in an excited, high-pitched voice. "I think it's something cruel to be alone in the winter. I bin expectin' Barney back cause he wrote he was comin'. Every stylish lookin' man I see goin' up the road I think, 'There's Barney now'. He ain't been back for two years."

"Leoda, you're sick and I am going to have Uly telephone the doctor's home," I told her. "And you'll have to go to bed or lie on the sofa."

"All right," she replied. Then she looked out the window and forgot her sickness for a minute. "Hey, Uly, don't you know you hadn't oughta stick the axe in the block? That's bad luck, that is." She sighed in despair. "There'll be no rest in this house for me or anyone else," she added wearily.

Uly went back home to phone the doctor and Leoda went on about her problems, but they were of such a nature I couldn't help in any way.

"I have to pay a fine too, and where is the money comin' from for that?" she lamented. "If it wasn't for Ida May, I'd take the days. Jail's not so bad, lots of pea soup and codfish in there. Only you have jailers." Leoda's eyes became dreamy as she thought of the past.

Then, as if the jail and hospital were closely related, she went on, "And I was in the hospital, too, twice. I had a leakerage of the heart, not very bad; then I was in when Ida May was born."

"Was that the Catholic hospital or the Prince Edward Island?"

"Oh, that was the Catholic hospital. They was good to me. I ain't complainin'. The Sister wanted me to stay there and work, but that was the time I had the leakerage, the first time."

"Well, Leoda I had better get you something to eat."

"Yes. I have some cans of soup and milk put away in the good room. I could take some soup."

As I entered the "good room" Leoda called out to me, "Them's pictures of Pa and Ma hangin' in there. We had them done before they went to Glory. I was glad we did. They're nice, ain't they?"

I noticed the enlarged photograph of a woman standing stiffly and dressed in a billowy, white dress while the man posed in the old style, with one foot crossed, trying to appear nonchalant. Everybody seemed to get great comfort from such pictures, and no home was too poor or its occupants too miserable to take an interest in family photographs. But there were also some breast plates from coffins inscribed with the names Moreena and Patrick Mooney, and some bright reddish hair framed under glass beside the plates. I supposed these were relics of Leoda's deceased parents, but I felt that to save such things was wrong and possibly injurious to one's health.

I shivered because it was very cold in the room. It was also used as a storeroom, and on a table, a pig's head was waiting to be made into potted meat or headcheese. She could get the head from a butcher for little to nothing but was obviously too sick to prepare it.

"And there's a phonograph in there." Leoda called out with pride. "We had some lovely records about how to look after your health, and another, 'It's Only One Step More.'"

All this was very dismal to me, and I began to wonder if Leoda ever got away from it. Did she ever have any social life beside the beer selling? I had never heard of her being invited to any social gathering. There was The Woman's Institute, but Leoda didn't belong.

"You can put on a record now if you like," Leoda went on.

"But I'd better get the soup now, hadn't I?" I said. I noticed that the phonograph was covered with a fringed square of chenille, and I thought it was probably broken and hadn't been played for years.

I hurried out to the kitchen while Leoda was resting. Ida May had finished her toilette and was running back and forth across the kitchen floor with her hands clasped behind her. She had probably seen a grown-up walk that way. As I watched her, I realized the child had been neglected and the mother uncared for. What could be done? Could somebody come and cook their meals? But who would come?

I supposed Leoda might be taken into the sanatorium

and Ida May to the orphanage. I would be glad when the doctor came to diagnose and give advice. Meanwhile, I would have to wash the dishes, tidy the kitchen and do what had to be done.

Just then, Uly returned. "I got the doctor on the phone and he said he would come right out. He had to go to the corner to see an old lady anyway."

"Oh, I don't think the doctor'll do much good," Leoda whined. "Did you ever try Pearson's Pink Pills? They're just great. I took them for a while. I would pin all my faith on them, but I am out just now. And there's an awful good medicine, they give it to the prize fighters to make them strong. Do you know what it is?"

I tried to remember what had been given to increase pugilistic efforts but could not think of anything. I was relieved to hear the doctor's car turning into the driveway.

"Well, well, Leoda. What is the matter here?" He greeted her as he removed sunglasses and peered at her intently.

"Well, Doctor, I am no damn good fur anythin'. I spit up some blood, but I thought perhaps just some loose blood somewhere. I didn't spit up much," she said apologetically.

After the examination, the doctor said, "I believe you'd better go to the Sanitorium for a while, Leoda. I think there is a spot on your lung and that is the place to be cured. "You may not have to stay very long," he added soothingly.

"But me poor kid. What's to become of Ida May? I can't leave her!" Leoda began to cry.

When Ida May saw this, she opened her mouth very

wide, revealing some decaying milk teeth and let out a loud cry. It may not have been a cry of desolation, for she was too young to realize what permanent separation would mean, but she must have sensed it. The doctor was affected too, by the tragic situation.

"Never mind, never mind, I think Ida May can go to the orphanage," he said. "I'll see if I can get her in and let you know tomorrow. Harold West had better come out with the ambulance, I guess. Your temperature is a little high to go all that way sitting up."

"But that is a hearse he uses for an ambulance. I don't want to go in no damn hearse until I have to," Leoda complained.

But the doctor paid little attention to her. He turned to me and I asked him if he would let me know when they were going, so I might come and get Leoda and Ida May ready. After leaving food ready for Leoda and her child, I walked home. The sun was going down, and as I passed a pond, it shone on the patches of floating ice and snow that reflected all the colours of the spectrum. The beauty of the earth continued unchanged, yet heartache and unhappiness were all around us.

The next afternoon, I was at Leoda's again because a message had come that the ambulance would be there at 3 p.m. I gathered their "best" clothing together. They seldom went out and all Leoda's clothing was old-fashioned, most likely hand-me-downs. I assisted her into a dress that was perhaps twenty years old. Ida May had a bath in the washtub, and she enjoyed the attention. When the time came for the coat and bonnet, she was well pleased. Her coat had buttons from neck to hem, but some of the original ones had been lost and bright ones of different kinds had been supplied. She was delighted with this and cried out with pleasure when she saw them.

At Leoda's request the previous day, I had decided to go with them. I had packed my suitcase and would head back to my rooming house after the case.

Leoda lay on a couch which had been put in for her convenience, and although she complained at first about a "damn hearse", she quieted down and went to sleep and did not waken until we came to Charlottetown.

Leoda was left at the sanatorium, much to the consternation of Ida May. I tried to comfort her by telling her that her mother would get well there and come back to her again, therefore we must hope for the best and be patient.

When we came to the Catholic orphanage, a Sister with a kind face and a sympathetic manner met us. She smiled down at the small Ida May in her buttoned coat with the red yarn still around her legs. I had an idea the yarn would soon be taken off, and I was glad I had thought of a doll that had been preserved from my own childhood. This I had brought with me and gave to Ida May. I told the Sister I thought the child's diet had been lacking in eggs, vegetables and fruit. Then I said my goodbyes and left.

From there, I went to register for duty and to see the nurses at the hospital. I was surprised to find some changes. Fisher had left and was doing private duty in the country, Martin was assisting on a case in the hospital, but Gillis was the most interesting subject of conversation. She had married almost immediately after she had completed her training and had gone to live in a distant town. Martin had the news that she was now expecting a baby.

Feed the Cluckers Before Night

A few weeks later, I had a phone call to go to nurse a Matilda Richardson who lived with her brother on a farm not far from the hospital. I had heard stories about the miserly ways of the well-to-do, eccentric old lady.

When I phoned Dr. Grant, I found out that she had quite a severe heart attack. He warned me that she would be what nurses particularly dislike – fussy.

Miss Richardson had had her own way too long to resist asserting her authority. She was a thin, grey-haired woman with a determined and often angry manner. Her bony hands, which were enlarged with blue veins, caressed the counterpane nervously. I felt her critical gaze, and when I raised my eyes to meet hers, they were cold and hard.

"Well," Miss Richardson said, "A big girl like you should be out planting potatoes. I don't think too much of all this sitting around dressed in white, but since you're here you might as well give me my cough medicine. It's

Coughalackin' and the dose is one teaspoon, so don't make a mistake and put in two."

When I brought the bottle of syrup, Miss Richardson snatched it, shook it vigorously and handed it back. "There now, measure me out me dose and be careful. Nurses often give the wrong dose. I heard of a nurse who did that and the woman died." When she had taken her medicine, she called out loudly, "Anselm! Anselm!"

An elderly man came in almost immediately. He was thin and grey-haired, but there was a twinkle in his blue eyes which made me think, although no longer young, he still retained the optimism of youth. He didn't seem to mind her scolding which began immediately following the announcement: "This is my brother, Anselm. Didn't I hear you stomping around the kitchen with them big boots on, wearing out the oilcloth and bringing in dirt?"

"Well, I took them off, Matilda," Anselm replied meekly.

"I should think so! The very idea! Where is Adam?"

"He is ploughing that piece of land we didn't quite finish last fall."

"Oh, Anselm! Get him right over there to fence the garden, before the cows get in, and, Anselm, go out and gather the eggs and see that the cluckers are fed."

"Yes, Matilda," Anselm replied as he leisurely left the room.

I soon found that Matilda constantly nagged the hired man. He was really the most criticized of the household, although the cook was a close second. Now, since Miss

Richardson was unable to leave her bed, she depended on Anselm's information. Why she disliked the poor young lad, I couldn't tell, for he seemed inoffensive enough and was still in his teens, with dark eyes and stiff black hair.

When I addressed him as Adam he said, "Adrian is me name, Adrian Leclair. I tol' her me name, but she crazee an' call me Adam. I not care, me."

I was relieved to see that he was as indifferent to Miss Richardson as Anselm seemed to be. He went easily about his work, usually whistling.

My greatest trouble was Matilda's drinking water. She refused to take water from the taps and demanded that I go to a nearby well in the yard for water needed during the day. There seemed no way to reach the water some feet below but to crouch down with a can suspended by a string and draw it up, full and overflowing. In this most dignified of professions, nursing, I found myself in so many undignified situations. I began to wonder what lady superintendents or head nurses would do under similar circumstances.

I was thinking along these lines that evening as I prepared to draw up the water when I heard a car motor on the quiet country road and wondered if it might be the doctor. I rose to my feet and was wiping the red soil from my apron when I realized that Dr. Grant was standing beside me. I attempted to look as professional as possible while carrying the heavy pail of water and made some attempt to greet him. He took the pail from me and said, "How are you getting along, Nurse?"

"Very well, but Miss Richardson is hard to please, or at least I find her so. Is she very ill?"

He responded, "Well, because of the heart attack, I wouldn't advise much moving around. I guess you'll have to humour her a bit."

While we made our way to the house, he asked if there was not a hired hand in the house who could draw the water. "After all, this sort of thing is not normally left to the nurse."

Matilda had much to say to the doctor in regards to her ailments and she looked curiously at me while I handed him the chart. I supposed she was wondering what I had written there, and perhaps it seemed to Matilda an under-handed way of doing things. What had I written? For so much could be said that way – she was being kept unaware of her condition. Despite her curiosity, Matilda was on her best behaviour until the doctor had left.

I was reminded of Dr. Grant's words about not being the hired girl later when I was preparing Matilda for the night. After she was settled in, she said sleepily, "You'd better go out now and feed the cluckers before night."

"That's Adrien's job, Miss Richardson," I said bravely. "My work here is to look after you."

In the night, I awoke from my bed on the couch and looked down at my sleeping patient. In the subdued light from a lamp in the hallway, I could see that Matilda's mouth was open and her upper teeth were exposed so that they appeared very large and long. I hoped she would sleep all night for if she awakened, she might demand unreasonable treatments.

From the window, I could see the light of the hospital in the distance. The operating room seemed aglow. Perhaps an emergency case had just been brought in. Serious nursing would be required if that were true. Some nurses would give gladly and cheerfully, and others would work perfunctorily. I feared that such would be the case with me if I continued to feel animosity for my patient. It occurred to me that I might become old and cynical in nursing and develop a stoop like Miss Sharp. I vowed to put any unkind thoughts out of my head.

When I awoke in the morning, although it was very early, Matilda was sitting up in bed, her pink shawl around her shoulders and her white lace cap on her head, with an attitude that showed she considered that the day had begun. She called loudly for "Adam," and although she called as loud as she could, her voice did not carry very far, and there was no answer from Adrian. "But it is early, Miss Richardson," I said. "It is only five o'clock."

"I know, but you call him, Nurse. I don't hold with laziness. He has to get the cows in and milked an' he has to separate, an' take the cows to the pasture before he goes to the fields! Get him up!" She was working herself up into a state.

I hastened to comply, knowing full well that Matilda knew her request would serve a double purpose, for I would be up for the day as well!

There was a sleepy response when I tapped on the door of Adrian's room over the kitchen, but when I was starting the fire, I heard him come downstairs, praying as he came. There would be no time to say morning prayers in his room, and Adrian seemed to be a devout Catholic who attended Mass every Sunday.

Feeling quite guilty about my irritation with Miss Richardson, I tried all that day to please her. At noon, I brought her dinner up on pretty blue dishes which I had found in the cupboard.

"Not me good blue dishes!" she exclaimed. "I never use them every day. I think the hot soapsuds'll fade them. And mind you, don't break them, and don't let the cook touch them. She already broke a dish. I heard a crash yesterday."

She always complained that her tea was too hot or too cold, and I wondered how long I could stand her steady stream of criticism. If I should lose my temper and quarrel with her, then what?

The cook became very displeased soon after I arrived because Matilda had complained that the meat hadn't been cooked properly. The next afternoon, I saw her prepare to go.

"There be's some that has property that thinks they can boss them that hasn't. Ain't that the truth?" she said to me.

"Yes," I replied, "but I wish you wouldn't leave. How will I manage alone?"

"Well, I wouldn't put up with it very long if I was you. You'll get no thanks. I didn't."

So I watched her leave, slamming the door behind her. She looked in the window as she passed and said,

"Tell her I've went."

Now we were left to cope. Anselm did his best to help by peeling the potatoes, making the beds, sweeping the floors, and cleaning the lamps. Since there was no talk of hiring another cook, I presided over the kitchen range which was fed with wood in all seasons. Coal was too expensive for Miss Richardson. I would run from the sick room to the kitchen, but they had not taught us to cook in the hospital! The gravy would not brown but would stay a greyish-white.

The neighbours were kind and brought in food of many kinds: bread, cake, jelly, and jam. But Miss Richardson ruled us all without leaving her bed. Like a puppeteer, she pulled the strings, and like puppets, we obeyed her. Although Anselm did not seem to hold her in awe, I saw that when she said, "That back field should be ploughed today," it was done, and although Adrian spoke of her contemptuously and said "She is crazee," he worked in the garden when she gave the command. And when she said to me, "Get me cold water from the spring," or "rub my back with the purple cologne," I did these tasks without question, remembering that the doctor had said, "Humour her."

I kept telling myself that I, too, should leave her, but then I had some pity for the other actors in this strange cast. It would be hard for Anselm and Adrian if I should walk out on them.

"You may as well give me my vilinary medicine now," she said, breaking into my thoughts, "and hand me the

Bam o'Gilead and the bottle of liveride medicine."

"Oh, but perhaps you had better not take a patent medicine along with the doctor's prescription," I warned.

"Well, maybe that's right. Might be poison together. I forgot," she replied. Then, since she could think of no other orders to give, she turned over and fell asleep.

One afternoon, after a busy day, I was considering wiping up the back porch. How much should a nurse do in a house? I wondered. The duties seemed endless here, and besides the housework, there were chores to be done in the barn.

Anselm had been working in the back field all day, so it fell to me to feed the hungry cluckers. When I had appeared at the henhouse door in the morning and the hens saw the white uniform, they flew into a frenzy of fear and tried to escape by flying past me as I stood in the doorway. That is enough of that, I thought, so I dressed for egg-gathering by covering my uniform with a long coat.

Matilda had been a dressmaker in her younger years, and this coat was a relic of bygone times. It had large puff sleeves and fit tightly at the waist. It reached my toes, as it had been made for a larger woman, and the double-breasted front was adorned with two rows of large pearl buttons. In this inglorious garment, I made my way to the barn when my attention was caught by unfamiliar voices.

Looking out, I saw that two women were walking up the path coming to call. They looked at the garden as they passed, and I heard their conversation. "Oh look, I can see the tips of spring flowers starting to come up," one said. "And Matilda's pink roses are lovely every year," said the older woman, whose wrinkled face brightened as she imagined the spring flowers in bloom.

"Yes. Matilda was always a great one for flowers," the other remarked. Then she saw me behind the screen door. "How de do," she went on, "How is poor Matilda? I'm Mrs. Hickox and she's Mrs. Sheeham. We was planning to come over for a spell to visit Matilda."

I let them in and Mrs. Sheeham came forward and shook my hand. I showed the women into Matilda's parlour and hurried to tell my patient of the visit. As I went up the stairs, I heard, "Oh, ain't them wax flowers grand! And an organ, too."

When I returned, Mrs. Sheeham was admiring the picture of Sir William Wallace in full military regalia. "Miss Richardson would like you to come up now," I said. I noticed that a small shaft of sunlight had crept in through the drawn blinds, making delicate patterns on the carpet and glorifying the roses and maple leaves in Miss Richardson's hooked rugs. She had always kept her blinds tightly drawn, lest her good mats might fade.

In the bedroom, there were the customary greetings. "Well Matilda, and how are you?"

"I'm a bit better, and how are you?"

"Well," said Mrs. Sheeham, "I've had the rheumatics all spring."

"Well, I had them bad this spring too, but I cured meself with Brudock Blood Bitters," Miss Richardson said with pride. "Show them the bottle, Miss MacRae"

A large bottle of brownish liquid was produced, with an engraving of a youth springing into the air to show that he was now relieved of all bodily ailments.

"How is Mary Lindsay? Is she any better?" Miss Matilda asked.

"No, she ain't a bit better. She has had the hiccups for fifteen years."

For the first time, Matilda referred to me, "What is the cause of that, Miss MacRae?"

"I don't know, but it might be some form of chorea."

"Well now, I bet it is," Mrs. Hickox replied, looking at me with great deference.

"Did you ever, now!" Mrs. Sheeham said and nodded her head in agreement.

"Well, I guess that's it," Miss Richardson said, in a tone indicating she considered the matter closed. She seemed to be used to dictating the conversation topics.

Then one of the guests broke in, "Did you come from Charlottetown, Miss?" Mrs. Sheeham asked. "I am planning on going to town one of these days. I want to get a hat to wear to Susan Mallett's funeral. I don't expect she's going to get better." She bowed her head and lamented, "We is all poor mortals."

"You make a cup of tea, Miss MacRae," Miss Richardson said impatiently, changing the subject again.

Over the tea, the conversation was resumed with more animation and various subjects came up, including some cases of illness.

Mrs. Hickox said, "Mrs. Alice Rodd got a terrible fright

this spring. It seems that a man was taken off of one of the foreign boats that come into Georgetown, and the doctors were afraid he might have yellow fever, so they shut him up in the hospital. John Rodd was working on the same boat. Well, one day the older children brought little Billy to Mrs. Rodd and was he ever yellow! He seemed to have a fever, too. She didn't know what yellow fever was like, but she was frightened. She was just going to call the doctor when she noticed that the bottle of butter colouring that had been full in the morning was almost empty. She got a basin of soap and water and the yellow soon came off!"

Then Mrs. Sheeham had her turn. "And Amos White is gettin' awful deaf. His wife will be calling him when he is out in the yard and he never hears her. So he got some good medicine, Fantix. It works two ways: there are pills to take and some ointment to rub around the ears."

I had little faith in such remedies. I felt sorry for these gullible people who were spending money on medicine that was worthless. "But that couldn't help him if he were deaf," I said. "Rubbing or pills wouldn't do any good."

The women looked at me in amazement. Finally, Mrs. Hickox said, "Oh well, it must have helped him because after he had taken a lot of it, he could hear a train blowin' a mile away."

"But perhaps he wasn't deaf in the first place," I said.

The women changed the subject and told how Amy Deloney finally got a man. Nobody had ever thought she'd get married, but she took a tonic called Supertanicus which "built her up and made her look real good."

As they prepared to leave, they promised to come again and said they had enjoyed their visit. Mrs. Sheeham's face was flushed and happy and Mrs. Hickox asked me to visit her.

Thinking of the patient, I suggested to Matilda that she rest after having company.

"Oh, it's only my first cousin, Mary Hickox, the only woman cousin I have. I have no sisters. She ain't poor, but I put in me will that Mary was to have most of me treasures in the parlour. I don't expect I'll get real smart again anyway, and the Lord only knows how much time I have."

In the days that followed, Matilda talked a great deal about the will and the fact that Mrs. Hickox and others might soon be enjoying her worldly goods. Anselm was seldom in her room long without hearing what should be done in the case of her death: what minister he should get, what hymns should be sung, what dress to put on her, and even the route they should take to the cemetery! He could repeat it all in his sleep, I thought as I listened.

One day, I smelled smoke and found that a small fire had started, possibly from wood sparks coming from the wood-box. I was soon able to get the fire out, but Matilda, upstairs in bed, smelled the smoke and became very alarmed. I ran to assure her that everything was all right and that only a little smoke remained in the kitchen, but her fear of fire persisted.

I was still busy in the kitchen and did not hear noises in the parlour where Matilda was working furiously. She had left her bed and was attempting to get her smaller possessions outdoors, for she believed the house was on fire. In the front yard, I found an exhausted patient stacking some of the smaller items from the parlour. The album on the brass legs, the big lamp, the sofa pillows were there, while the picture of William Wallace was off by itself under a tree as if looking out over the countryside.

"Oh, why did you do this?" I groaned. I took her pulse and it showed evidence of much strain. "I told you the fire was out!"

"Yes, I know you did," she countered feebly, "but I still smelled smoke, and it seemed to be coming up the stairs, so I lost me head, I guess."

I regretted that I had left her alone for I feared much damage had been done. This was the result of combining nursing and housework and I knew it. I propped her up in bed to make her breathing easier, but she was very pale and I decided to call the doctor. When I returned to the room, Matilda wanted to talk.

"I don't think I'll get over this. I feel so weak and sinking," she said. "I want to thank you for fussing with an old crank, Miss MacRae. I know I was mean, but I didn't feel well and then I thought nobody liked me, so that made it worse. I feel sorry now about the hired man. And him so poor, too." Her face seemed to crumple. "I think I'll give him some money. Look in that square box in the top drawer. There is a picture on the top of two hands clasped in friendship and there are some bills rolled up in that box. Give them all to him; I'll never use them now."

Her face moved convulsively and tears ran down

unchecked. I tried to comfort her by saying that I knew Adrian would be pleased and surprised to get the money, but nothing could comfort her very much. I got the friendship box and counted ten bills, each worth ten dollars. What a surprise this would for Adrian! But perhaps I should tell Anselm. He might consider his sister unsound mentally and might not approve.

When I told him of Matilda's wish he did not seem to care. "It's her money, so she can do as she's a mind to," he said. She never was very good-hearted. Give it to him."

That evening, the doctor came and held little hope for Matilda Richardson's recovery. When the evening chores had been done, I decided to present the money to Adrian.

He stared at it in disbelief. "She is crazee, like I tol' you. She must think she will die," he said finally.

"Yes, she is going to die, Adrian. The doctor says she will not get well," I told him. It was a shock, and something like regret passed over his face.

"Thanks. Tell her I thank her," he muttered. He spread his wealth on the oilcloth covered table and began counting while Anselm looked on, his eyes twinkling and a half smile around his mouth. "Un, deux, trois..." until he counted the hundred dollars. "I never think I have so much money, by damn," he explained, with emotion.

When I told Matilda about how her gift had been received, she seemed well pleased. "I must tell Anselm to see that he gets more, too. I am leaving more than Anselm will ever use and it might as well do some good. I believe Adam needs it. You see, Nurse, I had money left me when a rich relation died in the States. I never lifted me hand to earn it an' p'raps I might a been as well off without it. I don't know."

That night, Matilda passed away in her sleep without suffering. At once, the house was in a state of mourning, and she was laid out in the parlour where many of her treasures were being disposed of and carried away.

Mrs. Hickox took the big lamp, the album, and other parlour ornaments.

The picture of Sir William Wallace had not been claimed and Anselm said he did not care for it. "Shall I give it to Mrs. Sheeham?" I asked.

"Yes, if she wants it," he said and seemed to consider the matter settled.

Anselm had asked me to stay for the funeral for there had been many things to attend to.

The day of the funeral was sunny, and everybody concerned was pleased. "A rainy day is so lonesomelike," Mrs. Sheeham remarked as she came in the morning to help with the work. She was wearing the hat she had bought to wear to the funeral of Susan Mallet who was now feeling better and not likely to have a funeral just then. "But I am glad I got the hat," she said, happily. "I never thought of Matilda dying, but all them things is planned, I believe."

In the afternoon, a hush fell over the house as the funeral service began. I sat by the window and looked out at the red fields and the line of spruce trees that bordered the property. Some horses were tied to the paling fence and some to trees, for not all had come in cars.

With a look of complacency, Mrs. Sheeham seated her-self beside me. "There, think everything is tidy and ready. I went over the floor three times."

Looking at her, I had the feeling that she felt about the funeral as she would about any social meeting where friends gathered. She wanted it to be a success.

The minister was a tall, thin, nervous man, and when he began the service, he scarcely looked at Miss Richardson, beautifully and expensively laid out in a mauve silk dress, her white hair waved and a white peony in her hand. He began to preach about the shortness of this life and the endlessness of eternity.

When he was through, somebody played the organ and another rose to sing Miss Richardson's favourite hymn, "Shall We Gather at The River?"

I looked across at Anselm. He was very serious stand-ing there in his best black suit, but he would be too honest to pretend there was grief. I glanced at Adrian who seemed to be curious about the service and was listening intently and respectfully.

Mrs. Hickox was wearing a new outfit and she did not seem to be grieving. Mrs. Sheeham's eyes were red. She al-ways cried a little at funerals, and when it was over, she said to me, "That piece about the river flowing by the throne of God was so pretty I couldn't keep back the tears."

My work at this house was finished and I thought over the past busy, eventful days. It has been said that one comes closer to human nature in nursing than in any other work. How true that is, I thought.

More Goose Grease

A knock came to the door, and on the step, I found a brisk, business-like man who stood there looking me over with some uncertainty.

"Did you want to see my father?" I asked.

"No" the man said. "Is there a nurse here?"

"Yes, I am a nurse," I said.

"How do you do, Ma'am." The man lifted his cap. "My name is David MacMillan and my missus is very sick. Do you think you could come out and nurse her? We live about three miles from here and I have a good horse."

Yes, I could go. I prepared to leave with Mr. MacMillan, and I was also able to get Dr. Ryan on the telephone, who outlined what I should do for the patient. Several clicks on the party line told me that a good many people in the area would now be fully acquainted with the facts of Mrs. MacMillan's illness, but it was necessary to find out what I could about the treatment needed.

When I saw Mrs. O'Brien on the case, I was rather pleased. It seemed we were both being called on the same cases.

However, Mrs, O'Brien did not seem as pleased at seeing me and when she started to talk, I found she had lost all hope of the patient's recovery and was evidently trying to discourage me from the start. I had the impression she felt she could handle this case without the need for a trained nurse.

"Well, she's not long for this world, whatever the next will be. I got all the knickknacks moved out of the parlour in case anything happened," she said to me later that day in the kitchen. "I wonder what undertaker they will get. I like Burrywell meself, Glory be! They can fix you up to look grand though, an' reasonable too, considerin'! Me niece died an' she was the handsomest thing in her coffin you ever saw."

"But I think Mrs. MacMillan may get better. The doctor seemed to think so when I talked to him over the telephone," I replied.

"What did the doctor say?" asked Mrs. O'Brien," Did he say that he would change the medicine?"

"No, he didn't say. But he did say he would get some serum that might help. I think you give up too easily, Mrs. O'Brien."

I thought Mrs. O'Brien kept the patient too warm. I removed hot bricks and blankets from the bed after I had found Mrs. MacMillan's temperature very high. Then, I too, began to doubt that she would recover.

Mrs. MacMillan had had her baby before she came down with the flu. Many women who got the flu when they were pregnant did not recover. I wished fervently that she would, for it hardly seemed fair to die so young. There were few conveniences in this home, yet everything showed evidence of care and industry. There were several hand-made quilts, and on the floors, many hooked mats, while the sofas were covered with knitted afghans and cushions. I saw a picture that Mrs. O'Brien had moved from the parlour, but the pretty girl in the coloured drawing bore little resemblance to this thin, debilitated woman. I had the frightening thought of marrying and suffering a similar fate. It seemed as if my cases were designed to scare me away from the married state.

That night, I wrapped myself in a quilt of red and white squares and huddled in an armchair at the foot of the patient's bed. I had affected a cheerful manner, but now it was gone, and an anxious, miserable person struggled within me, threatening to take the place of the capable, efficient nurse. Then my patient woke, bringing me back to my duties.

She tossed restlessly, wildly delirious. "The water! The water!" she wailed. "Oh, I'm afraid I can't get the children across the water," she said anxiously.

"It's all right, Mrs. MacMillan. Here is a nice cool drink for you. Now, isn't that better?" I said as I turned the hot pillow.

"Please help me get them over. You know little Rufus can't walk very far." She moaned and twisted the blankets with her hand.

"Yes, I'll help you. Do you want another drink?"

Three o'clock. Would the night never end? At four, on taking my patient's temperature, I found it had fallen considerably and she seemed more comfortable. I stirred up the fires in preparation for the morning.

At five, a pre-dawn hush seemed to have fallen over the world. Although everything was as still as death, my patient was comfortable and I felt more cheerful. At six, the grey light of dawn began to flood the earth and a golden streak glowed across the horizon. Shortly afterwards, Mr. MacMillan arose, the children awoke, and Mrs. O'Brien started the breakfast. I could hear her singing "Til the Boys Git Back." She had just switched into "Tipperary" when I went into the kitchen.

"How is the poor woman this morning? What is her temperature?" She asked, wooden porridge spoon in the air.

From now on, much would depend on her temperature, which was hitherto unnoticed during Mrs. O'Brien's regime in the sick room.

"It is down this morning, but it will likely go up again this afternoon. It was a hundred and four last night," I replied.

"Glory be to God, and the Saints have mercy, Nurse, is it that high? What are you goin' to do, Nurse?"

"Give her a sponge bath."

"Lord, save us!" Mrs. O'Brien exclaimed. "Ain't you afraid she'll take a chill again? I washed her before she took so bad. If you wash her now and she dies, you'll never forgive yourself." Mrs. O'Brien watched me with some anxiety as I walked away carrying the basin. "Glory be to God, I'd rub her with goose grease until she's better," she muttered.

The sound of a horse coming down the lane alerted us to the doctor's arrival. Dr. Ryan came in, well bundled up against the cold. Although it was late spring and many of the farmers had already been working in their fields, the weather was changeable. This might be the "sheep storm" which usually came after the sheep had been shorn of their warm coats.

"How is she now, Nurse?" he asked, taking out an apparatus for a saline intravenous. "I didn't get the serum. There was none left in Charlottetown. Anyway, there is a good deal of doubt about its value."

The chart was examined, the intravenous given, and after what seemed a long time to those who waited in the kitchen, the doctor returned.

"Well, she is holding her own all right, but I can't expect much change yet. I will try to see her again tomorrow." Having delivered his opinion, which had been so eagerly awaited and on which they depended mightily, he departed in the mud-spattered horse-drawn wagon. Unfortunately for the doctor, the late spring snowfall meant impassable conditions for cars on the dirt roads, and he had many visits to make.

The following day, Sunday, there was not much change in the patient's condition, but she was no worse. The door of the patient's room burst open and three children entered. Loretta was eight and inclined to be boisterous. They missed their mother and they peered at the still figure in the bed, whispering amongst themselves. Already they had taken on a motherless appearance. Loretta's hair had been hastily brushed and looked unkempt. Johnny, seven, and Rufus, five, stood in even greater need of attention. Mr. MacMillan hastily herded them back to the washstand in the kitchen. Clumsily and with a heavy heart, he went about the motherly duty of getting them ready for Sunday School. "Do you know your lessons?" he inquired? "Get your papers and let's go."

Although I was in charge of the sick room, Mrs. O'Brien was still keeping an eye on my patient. When I next entered the kitchen, Mrs. O'Brien said, "Look, Miss MacRae, ain't you afraid to have the window open like that? Ain't you afraid she'll take the chill? That happened to Mrs. Dooley. They opened the window and she filled up, like, and the doctors had an awful time to pull her through. We all thought she was gone."

"No, I am not afraid. She isn't in a draft," I said quietly. "At least we can keep the air fresh."

"What is her temperature now?" Mrs. O'Brien asked, "Did you take it?"

"Yes, I just took it. It is a hundred and two, which means it is up a degree since this morning."

"Glory be, it is high, ain't it?" She was preparing parsnips for the midday dinner, but her face seemed strained and her hands shook, and suddenly I knew that Mrs. O'Brien was afraid. She was afraid of death in a way that I could never be afraid. To me, it was something that came about by natural causes, but to Mrs. O'Brien, there was something malevolent and mysterious about it, that could sicken a healthy person and bring them to death's door when they had been well cared for in every way. Mrs. O'Brien had never heard of Lister and his fight against bacteria and probably never would. Perhaps there had been too many flu cases, for Mrs. O'Brien seemed to be losing her spontaneity. She looked distastefully at some clothing I had brought down, and said, "And there's baby clothes to wash?"

"If Mrs. MacMillan sleeps, you can sit with her while I wash them," I said as I poured cold water, then a glass of milk and transferred them to a tray.

But Mr. MacMillan objected, "Can't you leave your wash until tomorrow?" He rose to go to the barn, and added, "You know this is Sunday."

I nodded, thinking that if he considered such things servile work on the Sabbath, we could manage. Mrs. O'Brien shrugged. Her church had never been so strict. On Sunday afternoons, the MacMillans could go out and enjoy themselves and this must have seemed like nonsense to her, but she said nothing.

Mrs. O'Brien slumped down wearily on the rocking chair in the kitchen and said "I must get off my feet for a minute." Her hair was disarranged and her face flushed from rushing. Now she wanted to talk, and that seemed to revive her.

"Do you know Mrs. Bradley that lives up by all them

poplars? She's had an awful lot of sickness. She had to go to Halifax. It was her pancreas, I guess, that bothered her. She was the worst colour before she went, all yellowish-brown, like. But when she came back, she looked great. They took it out, I guess."

"Took out the pancreas?" I was doubtful but trying to be diplomatic.

"Well, I don't know, but she says herself that she has all the parts she doesn't need removed from her – cut out. She had her appendix out first, then her gallbladder, then her tonsils. Ain't it a fright to have so many operations? And her daughter is like her, so much sickness. She has diabetes, but..."

Mrs. O'Brien was getting short of breath. I looked into Mrs. MacMillan's room. She was still asleep, but if she moved, I was near enough to be on hand.

Mrs. O'Brien paused for breath, then changed tack and said, "Look, Nurse, did you nurse a Miss Richardson? Somebody said you did. Well, her brother moved out a few miles from here. He sold the place near town that had been his sister's. Now he is married!"

"Married?"

"Yes, he married a poor widow woman from some-where. They say she hardly had enough to eat when he came along and he started buyin' her things right away. He bought her two sets of false teeth and gave her five dollars to buy a weddin' cake, and bought her some real nice clothes." She paused and I wondered could the poor widow be Mrs. Sheeham. I hoped that it was, so that the poor, gentle, sentimental Mrs. Sheeham could spend the rest of her days with someone as kind and generous as Anselm.

"Do you ever go to their house?" I asked.

"No, but you never know when I might go. Like I sez, here today and tomorrow cast into the oven."

"If you ever do go there, will you notice if they have a picture on the wall of William Wallace?"

"A picture of who?"

"Sir William Wallace. He is in battle dress with a helmet on his head."

Mrs. O'Brien looked at me with great interest. She likely had doubts of my sanity, but all she said was, "Yes, all right."

She went on talking, "There's a lot of girls in trouble this spring. More since the war. And they say Dr. Burke does abortions. He feels sorry for the girls and gives them something. It ain't right, though. I knew a girl – I'll not mention her name. They asked me if I knew of anything they could do. I said it ain't no use to ask me. I wouldn't advise epsom salts or tansy tea."

Looking at Mrs. O'Brien, I wondered if indeed she would resist advising something. It would not be like Mrs. O'Brien to be stuck for a remedy.

"...anyway, they got Dr. Burke, and the mother said she'd had a hemorrhage. And the girl was very weak in bed. You can put two and two together, can't you? I think I'll make a cup of tea. We was both up last night, and it helps if a person can't get enough sleep."

I agreed, tea would be great. Soon she returned with two cups of strong tea with a slightly boiled flavour and caraway cookies. The youngest child, little Rufus, also enjoyed the feast of cookies.

"These kids here are good. I was one place where I had a time, all right. I was like that old woman that lived in a shoe. They wouldn't do a thing that they was told. I stood it so long – then I just took down the Mary Jane and gave them a taste of it."

"And were they any better?' I asked.

"Well, yes, I just guess they was better! They knew they'd get it again if they didn't mind." Her thoughts turned back to nursing, "But isn't this flu terrible? All this sittin' around waitin', knowin' people ain't goin' to get better. So many deaths! They had a wake for one of my neighbours, an old man, that was. Everybody was sittin' around the coffin, and by three in the mornin' some of them were pretty drunk. The man that died had never been very smart, and they said he was lazy. Didn't one man say to the corpse, 'Get up now, and do some work, you lazy old divil!' At a wake, there is a lot of eatin' and drinkin'." Then Mrs. O'Brien stopped talking as if there could be nothing more to say and helped herself to another cup of tea.

Very soon, my patient stirred and woke up, and at the same time, there came a wail from a basket on the kitchen table – a decided call for food. We both hurried back to our respective duties.

Soon the children came in and were demanding cookies. Loretta was wearing a red and green coat with part of the hem needing mending. Her fair hair was a bit stringy. It needed washing, but she looked eager and happy with a mouthful of cookies. Johnny's overalls were just a size small for him, and his face was none too clean. He reached eagerly for a cookie, but a jug of milk happened to be in the way. It spilled, flowing rapidly over the cupboard and down to the floor.

"Oh Jesus, Mary and Joseph, look at that," Mrs. O'Brien said as she hurried for cloths to mop up. "Now we won't have enough milk for supper. Only one cow milkin'."

Johnny stopped and hung his head, fearful of what the future might hold for him.

Mr. MacMillan had just come in from the barn, smelling slightly of the stable. He had been cleaning out manure. He had heard Mrs. O'Brien's exclamation and shook his head sadly as if to say, "Not good for the children to hear profane language."

But all he said was, "See, what you did, Johnny."

Loretta felt that an older sister's reproof was needed for what had happened. "Oh, you bad, bad boy," she said. "Lucky thing for you that Mummy isn't up. Now you'll have no milk at suppertime. You'll have to drink water."

"Well, so will you," Johnny said happily as they went out.

When I took Mrs. MacMillan's temperature, it was a good deal lower, and her pulse rate was down too. She was definitely better.

"Do you know what, Mrs. O'Brien? She is better," I

said, smiling.

"And what makes you think that?"

"Her temperature. It is down."

"Glory be! I hope you're right, Nurse."

The following day the temperature was almost normal, and in the afternoon, the doctor verified what we were already thinking, that she was indeed better. I saw Mr. Boemer, a neighbour, and Mr. MacMillan talking in the yard and they were laughing. In fact, everyone seemed more cheerful.

They moved inside and Mr. Boemer now sat on the kitchen sofa. As the tension in the house had been removed, he relaxed and began a recital of his own family's ills and complaints.

I was doing up a uniform in the kitchen, as it was impossible to get laundry from the city, and I could not help giving advice as I ironed and listened.

"Me own Missis ain't any too good herself. She was awake all night with the earache"

"A drop of warm oil in the ear and heat applied should help that," I said.

Mr. Boemer appeared impressed and gratified. "Well now, is that so?" he said. "Tom has a sore finger, too and he is sufferin' a lot, but I think it is bealin' around the nail."

"He should soak the finger in Lysol and hot water. Lysol or sheep creolin; you know sheep dip," I suggested helpfully.

"Yes, yes, is it now? My word! Well now."

I was not quite sure whether all this appreciation was

sincere or if there was a note of derision in his laughing voice, but I didn't care. The good-natured Mr. Boemer went on telling how he had cured most of his ills with epsom salts.

"They're a great thing if you have a fever. Some try herrin' fastened on the soles of your feet to take down a fever, but I like the salts best, myself."

"Oh, that is just superstition about the herring," I told him.

"Well, I don't think so. I know what superstition is. My grandfather used to say that when a child was sick, they put the blood of a black cat on the cradle. But I know a good cure for jaundice, although you may not believe it," he went on. "If you go out in the yard an' see a flock of hens and see a hen with yalla legs, you catch it, kill it and drink the broth. It is a sure cure. My brother Tom tried it and he was awful bad. Even his spit was yalla. Well, he tried it and there was a change for the better right away. That's true, Nurse."

"I don't believe the colour of the hen's legs would make any difference," I said. I felt I must say something against such a foolish belief. After all, this was the twentieth century, not medieval times.

I continued ironing and thinking after Mr. Boemer left. Now that the crisis was over, there was one disturbing thought that persisted in my mind. I knew that Mrs. O'Brien had felt slighted when Mr. MacMillan had hired a trained nurse.

It was as I feared, for shortly afterwards, Mrs. O'Brien

packed her belongings. Although Mr. MacMillan offered her more money and asked her to remain just one more week to help him with the infant, she seemed determined to leave.

"But why do you have to go, Mrs. O'Brien? The case is not too hard now that the patient is better," I said, when Mrs. O'Brien came into the kitchen, her face flushed from her packing, and determination showing in the set of her jaw.

"Because I promised Mrs. McCarthy that I would nurse her. You know, they live in that grand big house up on the hill near town, and I want to be ready when they call. People like them ain't goin' to wait for a nurse. An' nursin' there ain't like nursin' in any poor place like this, I can tell you."

That afternoon, as I saw her drive off with Mr. Boemer in the buggy, I thought she looked angry. Perhaps she still felt that her knowledge and experience had not been appreciated when the MacMillans had brought in a trained nurse.

That night, the baby missed Mrs. O'Brien, or, in all probability, missed the soothing syrup and the pacifier, for it set up a loud wail at bedtime after it had been fed and diapered. Through the night, Mr. MacMillan walked the floor with the child, singing, "Must I Go Empty Handed, Must I Meet My Saviour So?" or "The Travelling Female Sailor." The crying would stop as soon as he began to sing. I was grateful because I was worried that the young mother would begin to fret about her baby.

In a few days, Mr. MacMillan found a woman who could cook and give Mrs. MacMillan all the care that was now necessary. They could get along without a trained nurse, so I prepared to leave. Mrs. MacMillan said she hated the thought of parting, and I was sad, too, at the time of leaving.

Labour Has Its Sure Rewards

I had another call to nurse a Mr. Angus Lynmore who had been stricken with pneumonia. The Lynmores lived in an area of the province which I knew to have poor farming land. It was a sunny day in May, and with the winter storms and blocked roads forgotten, I did not find the thought of another country case unpleasant. As we bumped along the country road in an old beaten-up truck, the birds twittered and chirped while nesting in the maples and alders. Many of the farmhouses were deserted, their doors hanging open and swaying to and fro in the wind. Soon the truck driver, whom I had asked to bring me, pointed up a rutted lane to a building near the road.

"That's the Lynmores," he said. "I'll carry up the suitcases for you." He glanced at me curiously as if to determine what I thought of the place, but I made no comment.

I watched him drive away as I walked up to the shabby grey house. It had a patched roof, and in one window, a piece of cardboard served for a windowpane. When I knocked, the door was opened only partially by a woman with suspicious dark eyes and untidy hair.

"Who are you?" she asked.

"I am the nurse, Elizabeth MacRae. Didn't you want a nurse here?" I was hoping after my first look at the place that they had changed their minds.

"Yes, I guess so," the woman answered, looking me over tentatively as she would a horse or a cow that she was thinking of buying. "Pa's awful bad and the doctor said we should get a trained nurse. We're nearly wore out, all of us. Come in. My apron ain't very clean, cause I bin takin' in wood. Sit down, Miss. You ain't had no supper so I'll get you something. Drink tea? I'm Sade, and it's my man that's sick and 'praps he won't get better. He was ravin' all last night. Joe and me was up with him. Joe's my son."

I ate my supper of smoked herring and bannock, and, because of the sickness, bought cookies. "No time to bake," Sade explained. The tea was hot and strong and Mrs. Lynmore took a cup herself. As we sat and talked over our tea, the door opened and a tall, thin man with protruding teeth entered. He did not look directly at me even when Sade said, "Here's the nurse, Joe." He walked to the stove to spit out a large mouthful of tobacco and a little of the juice splattered out on my white shoe.

He looked up at the dingy ceiling, and I noticed that one eye was partially closed. I thought perhaps that he had lost the sight of that eye. "How's Pa now?" he asked anxiously.

Mrs. Lynmore replied, "He's still sick as a dog, Joe. Sleeping now for a bit." Turning again to me, she said "And we worked on him in the night, every night rubbing him with goose grease and skunk oil. They say skunk oil beats the world for bronical troubles."

A young woman with a round, full face and bobbed black hair came in. Introductions were made quickly. I said, "I should go in to see the patient now."

The young woman who had been introduced as Sylvie got up quickly. "Do you want I warm the skunk oil?" she asked, her accent belying her French ancestry.

"Well, I would rather use camphorated oil for rubbing. Doesn't the skunk oil make a bad smell in the house?" I asked as I looked doubtfully at the bottles on the cupboard.

"Yes, terrible smell," Sylvie answered.

"But they say it's great stuff for the heaves," Joe said.

"Well, we ain't going to let Pa die for the sake of a little stink in the house!" Mrs. Lynmore declared with some indignation. "Use the oil."

I thought it better to let the matter drop for the present. It was always hard to shake people's confidence in home remedies. Later I would explain about the treatment in the hospital.

Sylvie followed me into the sick room and the room beyond where they had a bed for me. "Are you Joe's wife?" I asked.

"Yeh, Joe marry me in Mon'real when he's dere workin'. I no like dis dang place. Mon'real my home. He no like dere what you call ... man'ger? Lunch pail. He no like."

Just then Joe called loudly to Sylvie to throw out some turnips to the cow, and a minute later, I heard the turnips being brought up from the cellar under the house and thrown out the side door. This performance would not likely cause a problem to visitors, I thought, as I doubted that too many people would find this lonely place.

The inside of the house was reasonably kept and every room was papered with bright wallpaper. The sitting room was further adorned with calendars and a motto, "Labour Has Its Sure Rewards," done in red and gilt letters on a mirror. Calendars advertising patent medicines decorated the other rooms. One calendar showed a venerable, white-bearded gentleman surrounded by bottled medicine which he had made himself. Coming happily upon this formula, now he could help an ailing world.

I could hear Mrs. Lynmore talking to Joe in the kitchen with regard to sleeping arrangements, and her voice was loud and shrill. "She can have your room and Sylvie can sleep with me. You'll have to get along on chairs," she was saying, and in a lower voice, "An' I hope she ain't goin' to be too fussy."

I found my patient breathing hard, with a flushed face and a wild look in his dark eyes. I knew that this was not going to be an easy case.

Mrs. Lynmore had expected me to be "fussy," but she hadn't expected anything as extreme as splitting his shirts down the front and putting them on backwards.

"Well, Lord have mercy!" she exclaimed when I showed

her what I had done.

"To make bathing easier," I explained. "And do you have any sheets? Blankets are too warm when there's a fever. And do you suppose we could elevate the bed with blocks of wood?"

"Just as I thought," I heard Mrs. Lynmore say through the crack in the kitchen door which had opened again after she had slammed it. "She is a dammer to fuss! You know them new black shirts that Pa just bought? Well, she has them all cut up and the window is sky high! And I think she is goin' to wash him!"

That night, the patient coughed and moaned continuously. The cool spring air came through the open window. I wrapped myself in a heavy blanket in a rocking chair. Although I am not sleeping, I am resting, I told myself.

Sylvie came in to pay a goodnight visit. "Well, ain't dat hell, he so seeck," she said as she rolled a cigarette, crossing one foot over her knee in such a way that her knee was in no way elevated but made a perfect right angle, seemingly performing an anatomical impossibility.

In the sitting room, Joe had gone to sleep on hard chairs placed together to stretch almost across the room. He was tall and needed all the kitchen chairs.

The house became quiet and the patient tossed restlessly. Once Mr. Lynmore looked at me and said hoarsely, "Ya know, he buggered the car. He didn't look out and he had an accident. Careless. And another thing, pick your customers, I always say." He winked at me and repeated, "He buggered the car. Cost a hundred dollars to get fixed." He opened his lips in a grimace. Most of his teeth were missing, and although I had as stout a heart as most, the ghastly smile on the unshaven face made me shudder a little.

Almost no sound came from the wooded countryside, except the sound made by the cow as she nibbled the short grass around the house. Suddenly, I heard footsteps coming towards the house. I looked at my watch and it was two in the morning, very late for a visitor, I thought. Then a round fat face appeared at the open window. The man had a week's growth of reddish beard and slightly bloodshot eyes.

"How is Angus now?" asked the face.

"Well, much the same. Who are you?" I asked. It seemed the thing to say.

"I'm his neighbour, Jack Pollard. I just came home from town and saw the light, so I thought I would ask how he was."

Just then, I heard Joe rise from his bed of chairs and go out. A short time later, l heard the car motor and I knew he was driving away.

Dawn was streaking across the sky when Joe returned and took to his improvised bed again. I lay awake wondering what legitimate business he could have at this hour. I thought, perhaps, they are all thieves here. But the motto in the sitting room indicates that they believe in honest labour. In any case, even if they are thieves, they can't steal much from me, and no doubt they value my services because they seem to care for the old man. My fears were somewhat allayed, yet strange things seemed to happen in this house.

In the morning, Mrs. Lynmore, or Sade, as even Joe called his mother, bustled around getting breakfast. She seemed angry at times and rushed through the house complaining, "So much sitting around when there is so much to do!" She was apparently referring to Sylvie, who bothered little with the household tasks.

All day, the patient seemed the same; the monotonous, laboured breathing hadn't changed. Occasionally he looked up at me, his eyes rolling, and said, "He buggered the car."

The doctor came in the afternoon, just when I was ready for a rest. He was a short, stout, jolly man. How little there is to laugh at here, I thought, but the doctor seemed delighted, even when he went into the little room and saw the patient.

"I think he is doing as well as can be expected," he said. "You are doing fine, Nurse. Continue the medicine. See you tomorrow." When he took off with a great roar of his Model T engine, I wished for some of his optimism.

Then Joe came to sit with Mr. Lynmore, and I went to my room to rest. I was very tired, but when I settled in the old-fashioned feather bed, I was unable to sleep. Snatches of conversation floated up to me in Mrs. Lynmore's shrill, nervous voice, sometimes interspersed with swearing.

Later I heard a commotion and loud voices in the yard. I looked out and saw the Mounties. There was no mistaking their red-coated, snappy uniforms. They seemed to be looking for something, but not finding it, they left. At suppertime, I looked at Joe, but his face was unrevealing. There was no explanation and nobody spoke of the Mounties. I was curious and a little worried. Were Joe's late-night activities motivated by the need to pay the nurse? My straight-laced Presbyterian background made me uneasy to think that it might be so.

Another night came. At three a.m., I looked closely at the patient and noticed a change. A pallor had spread over the flushed face, the pulse was weak and the temperature subnormal. The crisis, and perhaps the end, I thought. My heart thumped. Stimulants and heat to the body, I told myself. I gave the medicine, then called Joe and Sade. Sylvie arose too and came downstairs.

"Pa is worse," passed from one to the other. "Perhaps Pa is dying," Sade's eyes were wild and excited.

It was customary in the country never to let the fire out when a patient was seriously ill, so I hurried to the kitchen for something that might take the place of a hot water bottle. I found hot hardwood sticks in the oven and I wrapped these in towels. I took the patient's pulse again and found it weaker. I thought perhaps Mr. Lynmore was dying, so I called Joe and Sade to come in. "He is very weak," I said. "You had better stay in the room."

Sade looked fearfully at her husband. "Yes, he is goin' now, ain't he? Lord, he's the colour of a corpse!" she said aloud.

Joe came in and removed the wad of tobacco from his mouth. It was his sole concession to the solemnity of death. Sylvie came in then, whimpered and stood with the others around the bed. Then the silence of death filled the room. I sat with my hand on the patient's pulse and as the minutes passed I looked at the wallpaper. It was white with blue flowers and birds. Bluebirds for happiness I thought, but how little there is to be happy about here!

Then I was surprised to feel the pulse grow stronger under my fingers, and almost simultaneously the patient's colour improved. "He is a little stronger," I said.

Sade bounced forward and peered into his face "He is better, ain't he?" she exclaimed. She began to cry, and Joe found his tobacco and put it back in his mouth.

The crisis had passed and it seemed the patient would be all right. Everybody was relieved and happy.

When the morning sun streamed into the room, the patient was still better and the various members of the family went about their activities with relief. I saw Joe give Sylvie some money and she was off to town.

From the kitchen came the thump, thump of the old stone churn. "Pa likes buttermilk and I thought I could get him some fresh, so I churned," Sade said in explanation to me.

But that evening, Joe and Sylvie quarrelled. They were in the sitting room and I feared their loud voices would disturb Mr. Lynmore. However, he was probably used to it because he just stared up at the ceiling with great complacency and called out only once, "Hold your gab!"

"I wish you would be quiet out there," I called to them. "You know Mr. Lynmore is still in a very weakened condition."

Joe looked up at the ceiling to answer, "Yes, Miss, I

know he is. Sylvie here. She's always complainin'."

That seemed to enrage Sylvie for she denied that charge vehemently and wished she had never come to "PI," as she called it. Soon, however, they declared a truce and decided to celebrate the old man's recovery. Several bottles of moonshine were brought to the parlour table, but Sade, exhausted, went to her room to sleep. After a time, Joe lurched to the door of the sick room, lifted his glass and said, "You fooled them all, Angus, you old son of a ...," the last under his breath as he caught my disapproving stare.

The next afternoon, when I took my patient's temperature, I found it much elevated and my anxiety returned. Had the celebration been premature? However, when I asked him how he felt, he replied, "I feel corkin', just corkin'. Guess I'll get up today."

I thought otherwise and was glad when the doctor came. If the doctor had been in high spirits the first day, he was now jubilant. He fairly danced with joy over his patient's condition. He did not think the high temperature was alarming.

Joe came in when the doctor had gone, and seating himself near the woodbox, looked up at me with curiosity and asked, "Why do you wear them damn white caps?"

"Well, why shouldn't we wear them? What have you got against caps?" I countered. Joe's resentment of uniforms was possibly the result of his frequent brushes with the law and his deep-seated dislike of law and order.

"Oh, they're just a way of being different and showin' off, I always think." He was trying to explain his attitude, and went on, "I was in the hospital last summer with me eye."

"What happened to your eye?"

"There was an explosion," He hesitated, then added, "In the stove. I was in for two weeks."

A car drove into the yard and Joe looked very uneasy. It was the Mounties again. I thought at first that Joe was going to leave by the back door. He seemed undecided but waited until two Mounties came in.

They looked over at Joe, and one said, "You have to come with us. We found the still in the woods, Joe, and Jack Pollard admitted that he was in with you." He seemed almost apologetic, as if Joe had been caught with his fingers in the cookie jar. Maybe they were being easy on him because they suspected the illicit money was needed for medicines and nursing care. Joe seemed as if he would deny everything but thought better of it and left quietly with the officers.

Sade and Sylvie seemed resigned as if they had expected this. Sade muttered something about "dirty crooks," and I felt sure that she meant the Mounties and not her son or Jack Pollard.

It was quiet in the kitchen for some minutes. There was nothing to be said.

The door opened suddenly and a small child came in without knocking. She was a friendly little thing and came to me, seeming to want affection. I noticed that her fair hair was covered with tiny white specks. She was infected with lice, but nobody seemed a bit concerned.

Sade whispered, "Yon's little Mary White from the

Tryon Road. Family's poor as church mice." She gave her a biscuit, which were freshly made every day, and the child devoured it quickly. Sade was being generous to her neighbour who had less than she, and not wanting to appear lacking in charity, I said nothing.

When Mr. Lynmore was no more in need of a nurse, Mrs. Lynmore found a man to drive me to the railway station, and I was able to make my escape. She had paid the going wage, digging the money out of a worn purse in her bedroom upstairs.

At the station, I found that the train was not on time, which was not uncommon. I sat on a hard bench and thought of how good it was to have summer coming. Nursing in winter was hard and I recalled the problems with poulticing in the winter. "Don't let the poultices get cold," said one doctor. He had his own recipe of linseed meal, vinegar, and onions all cooked together. Coming into a home when the poultices were being prepared, he would say, "that is a lovely smell," and sniff the air. "But don't let the poultices get cold. Change them often." That meant day and night duty for the nurse until there was a change in the patient's condition. Not many families felt they could afford two nurses.

When I reached my rooming house, I went right to bed. Rest was wonderful and I hadn't a care in the world. I decided to go home for a time, before taking on another case.

The next day I arrived home and found my aunt busy with house cleaning. Although I would have preferred to rest for a day, she decided that a papering project seemed of immediate importance and I must assist. While she carefully handed up the pasted paper, I stood on the stepladder and applied each strip carefully to the wall. While doing this, I became conscious of a terrible itching in my head. It was almost unbearable, but I could not drop the paper. Later I tried a shampoo with dandruff remover and on a sudden impulse, a fine-tooth comb. On using the comb, I found the trouble: while nursing at the Lynmores, I had been infected with head lice!

My aunt took in the situation at once. She, too, had complained of an itchy head, and now she looked at me with horror and anger.

"We have pediculosis," I said as I began looking in my case for bichloride ointment.

"You mean we are lousy!" my aunt said, putting her hands up to her neatly pinned hair. "Just plain lousy! This is a severe test of friendship, Elizabeth."

"Well, I am sorry, Aunt Mary," I said contritely. "I certainly didn't plan this, but I know all about curing it. I learned that at the hospital."

"Yes, you learned a lot at the hospital," my aunt said wryly.

We considered such dreadful experiences to be a part of nursing, and I carefully combed and cleaned with the powerful lotion until the awful things were gone. A sudden decision was made – my long hair had to go. Most of my friends had bobbed hair, but it was a momentous decision for me because my long, dark, curly hair was possibly my best feature.

Another Fall from Dignity

Soon after the Lynmore case, I was called to a case of diabetes. The patient, Tim Murdoch, and his wife lived on a road near New Glasgow corner. It was a pretty part of the Island. The yellow of the goldenrod, the mauve of the foxglove, and the blue of wild vetch mingled with shades of green along the edge of the road. The house was painted cream with pretty green trimming. It had a nice lawn and a few flowers around the door.

When I drove into the yard with the neighbour, Mr. Boggs, Mrs. Murdoch came out and took me into the house. She was a neat, thin, round-shouldered woman with a wind-reddened face and work-roughened hands. In the bedroom off the parlour, there was a large fleshy man with a very pale face sitting up in a beautifully carved antique bed.

While we were introduced, I noticed the perfection of everything in the room: the fresh snow-white linen on the bed, the patchwork quilts, the beautifully hooked rugs, and the highly polished furniture.

"Timmy took a bath before you came, Nurse, and I changed the bed," Mrs. Murdoch said.

"Oh, you should have left something for me to do," I said. It appeared that the red carpet had been laid out for me this time, and it was too bad because, outside of giving the insulin, there would be little to do. I wondered how I might put in the time and earn my money.

When I had given the medicine, I said, "Could I get you something to read out of the newspapers, or could I read to you?"

"A bedtime story, Nurse? That will be the thing," he said, laughing. "I never had very much time for stories. I've always been busy on the farm, but I read the Family Guide about the care of the animals when they get sick. I just had a hard time with a cow that dropped a calf up on the hill."

I guessed he had been seldom sick in bed and was unused to the general care given to bed patients, for when it was time for the evening ritual of the face and hand wash and the back rub, he seemed surprised.

After the wash, I opened the window of the sick room. Mrs. Murdoch was at once filled with anxiety. "Mind, Nurse, you won't let Timmy get in a draft, will you? He catches cold easily."

"No, I'll be careful. I can fix the window so the air will not come in directly."

Mrs. Murdoch seemed satisfied and went off to other

duties. Because of her husband's recent discovery of having diabetes, she was trying to do the many tasks in the barn and even in the fields, sowing grain and potatoes, with some help from the neighbours.

One afternoon, when Mrs. Murdoch had gone to fix a fence and Mr. Murdoch was asleep, a fish pedlar called. It wasn't my place to get supplies, and I let him go without buying. The fish man had only gone a short way when Mrs. Murdoch returned and was disappointed that she had missed him. "The doctor said that Timmy could have fish, and he can't eat so many things," she said sadly.

I considered Mrs. Murdoch's disappointment and I decided to follow him. I hurried out of the house and ran down the driveway. Even if I looked conspicuous, I wouldn't be going any distance, I thought. Down the road chugged the fish man in his old Model T truck with water dripping off the ice in the back, and down the road I followed. I overtook him as he stopped at the village store. I said breathlessly, "Can you come back to Mrs. Murdoch's?"

The fish man looked at me with curiosity. He tried to decide what should be done. Although chewing on a match, he still maintained a dignified stance. Finally, he said, "No, I'm not going back. I have just time to make me rounds and git back to the haying. But you could borrow a dish and take one with you." He nodded in the direction of the Post Office which was next to the store. "They will give you a dish or something there."

At the Post Office, in the front room of a private home, they looked at me curiously. Did I want mail, or stamps, or a money order, perhaps? No, I wanted a dishpan or something of that nature to put a fish in. I explained that I was nursing Timmy Murdoch, and I would also like to borrow some money to pay for the fish. From the back room where the family lived, the dishpan was quickly produced, and the money handed over the counter, with promises on my part to return it. They nodded sympathetically, wanting to help.

I was walking up the road with the fish, thinking that I had done what was best for the patient, when I noticed a car coming towards me. I thought, this is life! Yesterday, I walked this road properly dressed and in a dignified manner, and met no one. But now, dusty and dishevelled, and carrying a big codfish, I would meet someone. Should I drop the fish and if they should stop and ask any questions, could I pretend that somebody had carelessly left a fish in a dishpan by the roadside? No, I thought, that would be childish.

My heart beat a little faster for the car looked very much like Dr. Burke's. It was, and as they drove on, probably headed for Cavendish Beach (I thought bitterly), some girls in bright summer clothing looked laughingly out of the side windows. I supposed that this would be just another story for Dr. Burke to tell in the hospital dining room: "Say, whad d'ya know! I saw Nurse MacRae carrying a big codfish yesterday away out on a country road!"

However, the fish was greatly appreciated by Mr. Murdoch. He threw back his head and laughed heartily when I told the story. He rang his little bell and called out,

"Bring in some of that fish," even before it was ready to be served.

Many visitors came the following day, as it was Sunday, and Mr. Murdoch was delighted.

"Well, how is Timmy? I just heard he was taken real sick, and a nurse was here, too," said Mrs. Black, a neighbour. There was sympathy in her blue eyes when she offered to do anything she could to help.

Mrs. Murdoch told about the illness and how they had come to find out that Mr. Murdoch had diabetes. "The doctor says he may have had it for quite a spell because he ain't been feeling a bit well. I thought it might be his kidneys and I got him to take punkin' seeds. They say they're awful good for the like of that. But he wasn't any better so he went to the clinic and then to the hospital. At last, they found out for sure that he had diabetes."

"I brought over a little potted head, Bibiana," said Mrs. Black as she produced a covered bowl. "We killed a pig. Oh, it's not much."

"It's very good, I'm sure," said Mrs. Murdoch. "The jellied meat is just the thing for a sick man." Then she went to greet Mrs. Mullins who had just come in.

Mrs. Mullins threw back her scarf which had been wound about her head revealing a small, tight knob of hair on the top. It was a form of hair-dressing always suggesting the "ould sod." Her Irish face was alight with kindliness as she presented her offering, a large bottle of chicken broth. "Sure and the like will be good for him," she said, putting the bottle on the table.

The Women's Institute sent him some oranges and two young girls, their faces white with powder and freshly done marcel-waves showing beneath their hats, put down a bag of fruit beside the broth.

"Yous are all real kind, I am sure," said Mrs. Murdoch as she carried the food to the pantry. "I know Timmy will be pleased."

"Well, you were good to me when I had the flu," one girl said.

Soon Mr. Murdoch was up and around and I prepared to leave. I liked the Murdochs and thought that sincerity and kindliness were found to a greater degree in the country than in the cities and towns and that the country people were grateful for nursing. No doubt many nurses refused to come out from town because of the inconvenience and the loneliness.

Mr. Boggs was kind enough to drive me to the train station in Hunter River where I could pick up the train coming from Borden into Charlottetown. It was very crowded, for many were returning to the Island from distant parts to spend the summer months. I sat in the one vacant seat, but almost at once, a woman with several children approached, "Now what is the meaning of this?" she asked. "These are our seats. Didn't you notice our ticket stubs in the little box there?" Her eyes were angry brown slits behind her glasses.

"I am sorry," I said as I prepared to move. But the woman made a space on the seat for me. "Would you mind holding the baby for a minute?" she asked. "I have to make sure my crate of eggs is braced under the seat before the jerking of the train breaks all the eggs. She dumped a moist bundle of humanity in my lap. But when she had taken back her child, the other children cried for drinks of water, and she asked me to hold him again. Cookies were next and when a quarrel arose over these, I concentrated on the landscape. It was pleasant to gaze on the rolling hills with their pastel shades of rose, green, and mauve.

Later, she produced a bag of liquorice and the children settled down. The baby had never had candy and smiled in happy ignorance for a time. Finally, he began to cry, and although the mother crooned, he would not be stilled. She found a pacifier and the baby was calmed. But another problem arose: the children must be washed for the candy had blackened their hands and faces.

"I'll take them to the washroom if you'll be so good as to keep the baby," the mother said, looking at me as though I had been made for holding babies.

On her return, the mother asked, "Do you know what is good for the itch?" She showed me Anabel's hand which was scratched and reddened about the joints and where the fingers joined the hand.

"Yes, I believe it is scabies," I said as I examined the hand closer. "What did you put on it?"

"I put salt pork on it, but it didn't help much, and now I see the other children are getting it.'

"It is caused by mites that burrow under the skin. The doctor will give you something for it, or if you want a home remedy, a mixture of sulphur and lard will cure it;

but all clothing will have to be boiled or disinfected."

"Well, now!" the women said. "I don't doubt but what you're right." But her expression belied her words.

I felt I had introduced an alien note when I had used the technical term "scabies", and I was now under suspicion and was watched doubtfully as one might watch a foreign agent from a not too friendly country.

When the time came to leave the train, I found myself with the baby again, also the baby's bottle and a large bundle of diapers wrapped in a torn newspaper.

'Watch your step there, Missis," the train official said as he helped me down with my load. The mother followed with the other three children, and they found a truck waiting to take them to their destination. Finally, she took the baby.

"If you're ever in Thistle and Shamrock, ask for Mrs. Pete Pickles and pay us a visit. You'll get a good welcome."

I thanked her for the invitation but thought it unlikely that I would visit them, for I couldn't imagine a restful time with the Pickles.

When I walked down Grafton Street, I met Martin, who was on a case at the hospital, and together we walked to a square in the centre of the city. We sat on a bench and watched the fountain send out a scintillating spray, and I told Martin about the woman on the train. We had a good laugh over the incident.

Then Martin said unexpectedly, "Do you know, I would like to go to some quiet place for the summer where I could have a good rest."

This was so unusual for Martin that I looked at her in surprise. "Don't you feel well, Martin?" I asked.

"Oh, I'm all right, but I'm tired. I didn't rest when I left the hospital after training and I think that was a mistake."

"Yes, it was." I tried to see in the failing light if she had grown paler and thinner. Perhaps a little. Well, it was time to go to the restaurant for supper where we could talk about a vacation by the water.

A Summer Holiday at the Shore

In July, Martin and I found an old house for rent at a beach called The Cove. It was in good repair, but it had been closed over the winter and it smelled musty. But these drawbacks seemed trivial to us when we could lie in bed in the mornings and hear the splashing waves and plaintive murmur of sandpipers as they ran along the shore. We could watch the gulls as they circled overhead then swoop down to the sea. But above all, there was no exacting routine to be followed. Here, we could do as we pleased. We both felt a bit like wrecks that had been tossed ashore.

"I found that we can get milk and eggs from that big house on the hill, and they said that the fishman will come this way. At any rate, we have canned goods, and there is a store not far away," I said, happily planning the running of the household so that Martin could regain her strength.

We were just getting settled in when we heard a knock at the door. It was an Indian woman with baskets who introduced herself as Mrs. Lapine. I invited her into the cottage, and when she sat down, she glanced around and said, "You have no flowers in the room."

We had no flowers, but there were many things lacking besides flowers. Then I remembered having seen some matrimony growing, pink and white, in the neglected garden by the side of the house and made a mental note to get some and put them in the house.

But Mrs. Lapine had a definite reason for the flowers, for she went on, "I see the girl is sick and you should keep flowers in the room for the germ. You breathe out and they go on the flowers. I put them around my children when they are sick."

"What was the trouble with your children?" I asked, intrigued by this idea of bacteriology.

"I don't know. The doctor he no say. They cough and lie on the bed and then die. Seven die. All my children die," she said flatly.

Martin and I exchanged glances of pity and indignation. No doubt the children had been affected by tuberculosis, but she did not know that, nor did she realize how the white men failed them. We both knew of the Indian burial ground with the many graves marked with small white crosses.

When she learned that we were nurses, she thought of various bits of information that might be of interest to us. A Mrs. Bernard had fallen in the woods when she was picking mayflowers and had hurt herself so they had called Dr. Chumpin.

"Do you mean Dr. Champion?" I asked.

"Yes. He was the doctor at the place where she lives. She get all right but not go to the woods no more. Then Bodlich, her boy, take awful bad sick with the appendix and the doctor had to spleet him. He all right now. Her man was sick with the roomatics and the old Indian doctor come and said, 'I cure you.' He come again with pills and the man take the pills, but he wake in night with pain. His wife say 'Maybe you die, best send for the priest!' He say, 'No, I know that pills work,' but he stay awake all that night because if he die, he want to know it. But when he take all them pills, he cured of the roomatics. Indian medicine good like that."

"Have you ever lived at the reservation on Lennox Island?" I asked as she gathered up her baskets and prepared to leave.

"Yes. I live there for a long time but now living at Rocky Point. I live in house now," she said proudly. "You buy basket? Good for when you go to the store." Yes, we could each buy a basket and when the business had been transacted, she left. We watched her walk up the road, her bright baskets and flowing coloured skirt in contrast to her dark skin, making a beautiful picture against the trees and the blue waters of the Gulf.

"Well," Martin said. "That was a bright spot in what promised to be a very quiet afternoon."

"Yes, indeed. Now I am going down to the spring for water," I said, "and I may get some firewood while I'm out."

Out in the grass, I found a little bird that seemed unable to fly. I took it home and Martin and I undertook the nursing care. The feeding was the greatest problem, as it seemed so many worms were needed. As the days passed, the bird grew weaker, and in the morning, the question was not, "How did you sleep?" but rather, "How is the bird?" However, the bird did not recover and Martin said I hadn't given it enough worms.

Our next case was a young crow with a broken wing. We put him in an empty room with water and food. During the day, he stepped around happily enough, with no apparent thought of evil in his little black head, but at night the mess and destruction he caused were almost more than we could cope with.

The next morning, I received a message asking me to go back to the hospital at once. I had mixed feelings about it. Should I leave my friend? Why should I give up my holiday? I opened the door and looked again at the room that the crow had made so uninhabitable. How could I leave Martin in a weakened condition to clean up this mess? I told the neighbour who had come with the request that I would not be able to accept the case.

In a couple of days, when we grew tired of lounging around and reading, we walked along the beach where uneven masses of rose and purple-shadowed rocks jutted out into the sea. We saw two people coming across the sand towards us. At first, we thought they were fishermen looking over some lobster traps that had been washed ashore. Then we saw that they were not fishermen. They were Dr. Grant and Dr. Burke, and they brought the hospital very near again.

They explained that they had been passing this way and thought they had better inquire after Martin's health. It was also an opportunity to enjoy the sunshine, as they had been indoors a good deal.

They sat and talked for a while until the tide lapped at our feet, and I wanted to gather some driftwood and go back to the cottage and prepare supper. The doctors helped us to gather up bits of broken lobster traps and small sticks scattered along the shore and then walked back with us. Dr. Grant appeared out of his element, holding the sandy wood carefully in his surgeon's hands and as far as possible from his immaculate clothing. Dr. Burke seemed happy and relaxed, feeling at ease because country life suited him.

Since the doctors had helped with the wood, and it was time for an evening meal, it seemed only courteous to ask them to stay and eat with us. My invitation was accepted readily. I lit the fire and started supper.

Our drinking water was our greatest problem. There was an old pump nearby, but the water we pumped was always coloured with the red soil of the land. Said Martin, "Well, it is good and rich looking. They say variety is the spice of life, so we may as well have it highly coloured when we have the opportunity." The alternative was to go to the spring. The water there was clear, but flies and bugs seemed always waiting to enter the bucket and float gaily around on the surface. I decided to get some water from the spring, and as I entered the kitchen, Dr. Grant rose at once to take the bucket from me. When he saw the flies, he was horrified, as I knew he would be. "Do you boil your water?" he asked anxiously as he lifted the bucket to a shelf.

"Yes, but usually we drink tea and ginger ale," I said. I felt I was back in the hospital being cross-examined about a treatment.

Dr. Grant worried about getting ulcers as he sat down to a supper of sardines, bread, cake and fruit. He sat up straight and unrelaxed. Even here at the shore where the setting was so informal, he couldn't seem to feel at home.

Dr. Burke sat on a keg, his large body bulging over the edge, and talked about a patient. He said he had a case of plural pneumonia where the temperature went down, but the pulse and respirations never became normal.

"My Lord, man, don't you think you should have aspirated?" Dr. Grant asked.

"Not according to the rules, I shouldn't," said Dr. Burke.

"Well, I had a case not long ago where another doctor helped me. It was in the country and the patient recovered in a short time," Dr. Grant said, forgetting his supper in the urgency of the discussion.

Martin looked amused, but I thought it too serious and wondered what I could say to turn their minds to a brighter topic. "We have a crow," I said, as one would announce a rare item of news.

"A crow?" they repeated in unison.

"Yes. We can go to see him when we are through supper," I said. I was surprised at their interest and grateful for an abrupt ending of the argument.

Soon the doctors were peering in at the crow, much as they might look at an interesting case, while the object of their scrutiny, with a distrust of humans caused by unpleasant associations in the past, stepped warily to the far end of the room.

"Once I had a crow that was like a blood brother to me," Dr. Burke remarked. "You see, we got him when he was very young and he sort of grew up with us. No matter what we did, he was there. When we ate our meals, he waited to be fed."

"What happened to him?" Dr. Grant asked with interest.

"Well, he just flew away, I think. One day, there were a lot of crows around and they coaxed him away. I wonder how crows would do to experiment on instead of guinea pigs!" mused Dr. Burke.

"Well, they have been used," interjected Dr. Grant, and he continued to detail his knowledge on the subject. "All animals have been used, from the amphibia to highly developed mammals. In the study of the nervous system, the behavioural development of birds has been noted. The pecking of chicks was considered from the maturational standpoint, and it was shown that both physiological factors of maturation and the effects of exercise are at work. It was found that young chicks, given their first chance to peck, always start out with a poor score, while those which are older on their first attempt do much better."

I laughed but he went on. "The amphibian amblystoma is especially suitable for experimentation because it is independent of its mother from the gastrula state on. It has the advantage, like an amphibian, of growing appendages for use in quadrupedal locomotion typical of higher animals."

"Sez you!" Dr. Burke scoffed. "You have read up on that because you are lecturing on the nervous system."

"So, you are feeling stronger?" Dr. Grant asked, changing the subject and turning to Martin. "You will gain down here. The ultraviolet rays will increase iron, phosphorous and calcium in the blood. This place is better than an iron tonic. We must come down here again soon, don't you think?" he added, looking at Dr. Burke.

Dr. Burke thought the idea of coming again was wonderful. In fact, they may even come tomorrow. This was a slack time at the hospital and as long as the weather continued, why not enjoy it?

The next day when the doctors came, we all went out gathering dulse. Martin and Dr. Burke ate it and enjoyed it, but Dr. Grant and I declined. Here was one thing we had in common!

"Hey, Grant, don't you know all the medicinal qualities it contains?" Dr. Burke laughed uproariously as he offered him some of the seaweed.

We ate sandwiches and fruit and drank ginger ale which had been supplied by the doctors. We lingered on the beach until twilight when everything was still. Even the birds were silent, and the landscape was bathed in a pink light from the reflecting sun. When the tide was going out, Martin and Dr. Burke went to look for clams.

But Dr. Grant's mind had gone back to the hospital. "You remember that young man in number one, the one who had us all baffled as to what was wrong with him? Well, I found out he had worms. You never guessed that, did you?" He looked searchingly at me.

"No, I didn't," I answered. But I thought that the evening was too nice to talk about such things. Worms! How dreadful!

"I treated him and he was all right in no time," he went on.

"Good," I said without enthusiasm.

Taking a stick and tracing letters in the sand, he said, "I am planning on going to Europe to spend some time at a hospital there. I will be leaving soon and Dr. MacLeod will take my patients for the next while. I am not sure; I may be gone for a few months."

"You are?" I was astonished.

"Yes, and I trust you won't leave here. I hope to have you on my cases when I get back. I need you as well as my patients."

I said nothing. I felt disoriented. I had never thought of Dr. Grant leaving, but the rebellious thought came to me that travelling seemed to be a male privilege. Despite the closeness that had developed between us, it seemed that what he wanted was total dedication from me so that he could pursue his career to the fullest. I wondered whether we could ever be compatible.

We walked in silence back towards the house where we found that Martin and Dr. Burke had steamed the clams over the open fire in a clam pot borrowed from our neighbour. The sight brightened my mood, and I was content to listen to Martin's stories and the laughter of Dr. Burke. Soon afterwards, the two men thanked us and said their goodbyes.

Martin gained steadily and soon felt her strength had returned so she could go back to the old routine. We closed the old house with the hope that we could come again another summer.

No Medicine
from a Spy

When I went to the telephone, Miss Eden, the matron, was on the line. "Miss MacRae, Dr. Dennis telephoned that he wants a nurse to look after a Miss Laurance. It's on the outskirts of the city. She has nephritis, but it seems she has developed a mental condition and needs a great deal of waiting on. The doctor thinks that her mind will clear when her physical condition improves. He did not seem to think that she was a case for Oakwood, and anyhow, I couldn't get one of their nurses to come. Will you go?"

I hesitated before replying, "Yes, Miss Eden, I'll take down the number. I shrank at the prospect, but one didn't refuse Miss Eden easily. Coolly remote in starched perfection, she always seemed to expect a great deal from her nurses.

With some apprehension, I took a taxi to Miss Laurance's house. The taxi driver waited a minute while I made sure of the number, as the house was set from the street and surrounded by trees. It looked mysterious and lonely with many wings and gables. Some blinds were completely down, while others were at half-mast. The whole appearance of the place was uninviting, and I was conscious of a feeling of distaste and dread.

A middle-aged woman with a flushed face answered my knock. When she saw that I was the nurse, her expression changed. "I am so glad you've come! I can't get a thing done with my sister wanting so much attention. There, she wants me now. All the time it's like that," she said, almost in one breath.

I heard a knock, knock, knock as if made by a metal object on glass, then an anxious call, "Jane, will you bring me a glass of water?"

"Yes, yes, I'll be there in a minute. Your room is upstairs at the right, Miss MacRae," the patient's sister said hurriedly as she went to the sickroom.

When I entered the patient's room, I raised the blind that I might better see the woman in bed. She was wetting her face with little pads of absorbent cotton which she moistened in a bowl on the bedside table. Some of the water clung to her untidy hair and her flushed face. Because of her mental condition, her dark eyes looked wild and restless. She peered up at me through her dripping hair and said, "Can you bring a drink of water?"

I brought the drink and was surprised to see my patient test it with her finger. It seemed she wanted the water at room temperature, and it was hard to get the exact warmth to satisfy her.

Her sister came in with a pitcher of hot water and handed a glass of cold water to me. But although we tried to mix the water to suit Miss Laurance, it was either too hot or too cold. And she needed to drink plenty of water.

Later, I saw her surreptitiously take the glass and drink long and thirstily. Unfortunately, the drinking water wasn't the only problem. She wouldn't consent to me giving her a bath, nor would she take her medicine. She said the medicine was salty, and she was thirsty enough without taking salt.

Miss Laurance's mental state changed quickly. When she was supposed to be sleeping in the afternoon, she sat up quickly. "Can you add two and two? she asked, raising herself on her elbow. "I can never get it to come out right now. It will be either five or three every time." Then she thought of the drinking water, and we were back to the old routine.

Dr. Dennis had said he would call that afternoon, and it seemed to be an event for which Jane prepared industriously by sweeping, dusting, and changing the bed linen. The difficulty with her sister, Abbie, was that she would not be "fixed up." "She's a sight," Jane said as she put her best crocheted spread on the bed. The reason for all this preparation sat in her pretty bed, unwashed and uncombed, with a sullen expression on her face and dripping water on the hemstitched sheet.

Jane left the room and returned in a short time "dressed." She had frizzed her hair in an old-fashioned way about her face and had put on a loose, full-skirted dress that reached to the tops of her high-laced pointed-toe shoes. That had been the style of dress when she was a girl, and to add a finishing touch, she had pinned a small watch with a fleur-de-lis pattern to her high-necked blouse.

This way of dressing and other things about the house convinced me that the two sisters had remained static in a changing world.

It was nearing suppertime when Jane ushered Dr. Dennis into the sick room. He was a large man with long white hair, and when he removed his glasses to wipe them, I noticed dull, faded blue eyes. He was wearing a cut-away coat, a style seldom used by Island doctors, but I believe affected by some in Europe and other countries.

"She wouldn't take her drinks or let the nurse bathe her," Jane complained, ignoring the chart the doctor was reading. "Nor her medicine. She wouldn't take that either," she went on.

But Abbie allowed a stethoscopic examination of her heart and lungs, and Dr. Dennis had done a urinalysis which pleased him very much.

"Give her that bromide mixture and she will be all right, Nurse," he said

"Yes, if I can get her to take it," I said doubtfully.

But he seemed unworried about what seemed inevitable to me. He sat in a chair, his stethoscope about his neck, repeating, "She'll be all right now, she'll be all right," as he stared up at the ceiling. I thought he looked like the Mad Hatter in his cutaway and that he blended into the atmosphere of the place very well.

"And she hasn't eaten anything for two days," Jane said as she fingered the fleur-de-lis pin nervously.

"Yes, but I see by the chart she has taken a good deal of milk," the doctor returned. He rose and added, "I must go along now, but I think she'll be all right."

But she wasn't all right. Her mental condition remained the same. That evening when the lights were on, I looked out the window and saw there were no close neighbours. The nearest light must be a block away, and I began to wish for the security and companionship of the hospital. As one remembers only the good in the character of a deceased or departed friend, there now seemed only desirable qualities in the hospital and its staff. I had to admit that there was even good in Miss Eden, who had executive ability and could keep things going, and in Miss Sharp, with her old body that had grown misshapen in the service of mankind. And if anything went wrong, Dr. Burke was on duty or on call, always dependable. Most of all, I missed the camaraderie of the nurses.

Although a sofa was prepared for me, I had little chance to rest because when I went to lie down, I would hear almost at once, "Nurse, will you get me a drink of water?"

At last, having exhausted herself, Miss Laurance fell into a sleep, longer and deeper than usual. I slept but was awakened by someone in white standing by my sofa. Abbie, was my first thought. My heart almost stopped and I found myself unable to move, but then I saw that the spectre was really a much older lady in a white nightdress. "Who are you and what do you want?" I asked.

"My name is Melissa Laurance. I would give you my calling card if I had one with me," she said acidly. "I want my cat, Tabby. Who are you?"

"I'm the nurse."

"Nurse?" she repeated. "Who did you come to nurse?"

"I came to nurse Miss Abbie," I said, looking in the direction of the bed where Abbie slept.

"You did? And there's nothing in God's earth the matter with her, is there, Nurse? She's just acting up, isn't she?"

"No, she is really quite ill," I answered.

"She is?" Then the old lady lowered her voice and whispered, "Do you know of anything that is good for corns?"

I looked down at a pair of fat, bare feet but could see no sign of corns. When I realized that she was not going to let me sleep, I said, "I'd like to go back to sleep now while Miss Abbie is resting. I'll take you to your bed."

"I'll go in a minute." The old lady walked over and looked down at the sleeping patient, and then turned to me. "Well, give me a bath and make my bed, if you are a nurse."

"I will tomorrow," I said and escorted her back to her room.

The next day, when I told of my midnight visitor, Jane said, "Yes, it was Aunt Melissa. She is quite harmless. You need not be afraid of her, but I should have warned you."

The next night, I again slept in the room next to Miss Laurance. Once, as I looked in on her, she said, "Yes, I see you, you little blue-eyed devil! You are spying on me!"

There were glass doors at the other end of the patient's room and I reasoned that it might disturb Abbie less if I were to creep around and look in through the small panes. I did so later that night, and when I lifted my face to the pane of glass, there was my patient peering out at me, her face pressed close and her hair standing out in little braids at each side of her head. And in the dim light, I could see that she was angry. "Spying on me!" she said scornfully.

In the morning, Miss Laurance told her sister that she would take no medicine from a spy. "You go home," she said.

I wondered what I should do if my patient became more unmanageable. Would her sister, Jane, hear if I called? The best plan, I thought, was to leave Miss Laurance alone and perhaps she would quiet down and go to sleep. I began to look for a good book in the bookcase which Jane had told me I might enjoy. I heard a noise, and when I turned, suddenly Miss Laurance was coming towards me angrily with a water pitcher in her hand. The jug was empty, but I feared Abbie intended breaking it over my head.

"Jane, help!" I cried, but my voice seemed small and weak and in no way equal to the emergency. My training had given little help in regard to handling mental patients. I must show my authority, I thought. As firmly as I could, I said, "Go back to bed, Miss Laurance!"

I thought she was going to obey when she put the jug on the table, but she suddenly grabbed my arms and turned me around. She was strangely very powerful and I had thought her so frail. She took me by the shoulders and it seemed she planned to push me out of the house.

Through misty eyes, I saw the old lady again, standing in the doorway in her white nightdress. Her round pink face showed only placid interest. There was no alarm in her vacuous eyes.

"Get help," I croaked hoarsely as the old lady continued to watch. Then I saw the crockery jug lifted over my head and everything went black.

When I opened my eyes, Jane had come to the rescue. The old lady had at last given the alarm and Jane had rushed in. I was able to stagger to the sofa, and at Jane's request, the old lady brought me a glass of cold water.

Miss Laurance was very meek now for she had heard Jane say that she must be sent to the mental hospital, Oakwood, and she was shocked into reality.

"Don't send me to the 'sylum," she begged. "I'll be good. I'll be all right now."

"I can't look after her." Her sister spoke as though talking to herself, her shoulders shaking with emotion. "She has been violent, and I can't expect a nurse to stay with her. I see no help for it. She must go and the doctor must come to make the arrangements."

When Dr. Dennis arrived, Jane welcomed him with little ceremony. "We have had trouble here, Doctor," she said.

Abbie looked up at him with a chastened, frightened expression but said nothing. I pushed the chart up to him, expecting some indication of surprise or regret, but there was neither in his countenance. Nothing marred the passivity of his features.

"Did you give her the bromide?" he asked me, peering

at her over his spectacles.

"No, she wouldn't take it." I answered.

"She struck the nurse with a jug, Doctor," Jane said, "and now she must be sent to the asylum. Will you make the arrangements, please?"

"Yes, certainly. I'll just fill out these papers." He sat at the table to write, his white hair falling over his face, his hand trembling as he worked.

"I wish you would order something for Aunt Melissa so she will sleep better at night," Jane said, coming over to the table and addressing the doctor. "Between the two of them, the nurse has been frightened out of her wits."

"Yes, I'll give a prescription for some luminal. That should help her," he said.

I looked at Jane's worried face and pitied her. Of all those involved, she was probably the one most deserving of sympathy, having to care for two mentally unstable and troublesome patients.

The next day, I assisted Jane with a protesting Abbie. "Oh, don't send me to the 'sylum," she said over and over again. But Jane was adamant and poor Abbie was led protesting to the car. When we were leaving, I looked back and saw the old lady at the window. She looked mildly curious, her white hair fluffed up like a halo around her face.

"You are not taking me to Oakwood!" Abbie said as we drove off. And even when signs said with sad certainty, "Oakwood," she kept begging, "Oh, don't take me to Oakwood!"

Abbie went into the building unwillingly, but I thought

that when we met the nurse at the desk, she was trying desperately to be quiet and composed. "I am not insane," she said to the woman who came forward and put a friendly hand on her arm.

"No. We never use the word 'insane' here, but I can see you are nervous and upset. Don't worry," she said, "we will do all we can to help you, Miss Laurance."

They walked down the corridor to a pleasant room with frilly curtains and cream-painted woodwork. There, we left Abbie with the nurses and walked away. Jane was trying not to weep, and when the car drove down the tree-sheltered paths, she dried her eyes.

"We could do nothing else. She will have treatment here," she said.

I noticed that Jane hadn't frizzed her hair nor had she worn the fleur-de-lis pin. In the extremities of sorrow, people care little about appearances and in her neglect for herself, Jane proclaimed her grief and pity for Abbie.

My case was over, and in light of what had happened, my effort hadn't helped. But that was past. I said goodbye to Jane, and the obliging neighbour, who had taken them to the hospital, took me to the store in the downtown area and left me there. The goods on display meant little to me, for when the clerk said, "Something I can do for you, Miss?" I heard instead, "No, you're not taking me to Oakwood!" I thought this over and decided it was not wise to be too affected by the emotions of other people if I were to do my best work. But I was depressed and could not concentrate on purchasing anything that day.

I phoned Miss Eden and explained about the case and how I had come to be free. She did not seem surprised or sympathetic. Perhaps she thought I might have managed better and not let Miss. Laurance get the best of me. Matrons were sometimes like that, expecting the impossible.

I was tired both mentally and physically, but it was Saturday, and I could go home for the weekend. I had only to gather a few things from my rooming house and catch an afternoon train.

When I walked home from the station, my father was busy at the barn, and on seeing him, a flood of happiness came over me. Close association had always prevented my seeing him as he really was. Now, from the vantage point of maturity and experience, I saw a thin grey-haired man, with shoulders stooped by hard work and heavy lifting. If judged by earthly standards, he might not be considered a success. But he had taken the place of a mother who died young, and now his welcoming smile was encouraging and comforting. I answered his inquiries about my health, my cases, and the room I had found in the city. Then we walked past some lilac trees into the house.

My Aunt Mary came in and wanted to know about my case and how I had managed. She was very efficient, and I had often wished that her eyes were less keen, less quick to notice what, according to her standards, she considered not to be quite correct. An imposing figure, she liked to be thought plump, not fat. She usually wore well-starched, frilly aprons which added a bit to her size.

"My patient has gone to Oakwood," was all that I

could say.

"To Oakwood? Why? Was she crazy?" Aunt Mary was greatly interested. Next to murder and rape, a mental case was a good conversation topic.

"Yes, she struck me with a jug," I said.

"But why did she strike you?"

"Well, she was all mixed up. She couldn't come to terms with reality."

"You are too small to nurse anyway, Elizabeth. You need to be big and have big strong arms like Mrs. O'Brien. She is a good size and her patients trust her," Aunt Mary said decidedly.

"I don't think size has anything to do with trust."

Then she thought of my new blue suit that had just come from Eaton's. "But I am afraid that the skirt is too short, Elizabeth, the dresses are so short now, ever since the war. Too short. It's disgraceful. I hope you won't follow that fashion. She looked critically at my skirt to see if it had indeed risen above the bounds of propriety. She then took up her crocheting.

The window was open, and looking out across the fields, I could see that some farmers were still out working. There was the everlasting list of duties: weeds and insects to be destroyed, fences and equipment to be repaired, ailing animals to be restored to health, trips to be made to stores for supplies. But overall, there was the quiet and peace of the country. The scent of flowers came in from the small garden patch by the paling fence. Then the slanting rays of the setting sun caught the colours and made them even more brilliant.

"Your flowers are very pretty, Aunt Mary," I said. Flowers were always a pleasant subject of conversation.

"Yes, they are a good deal of work but they are worth it. Uly brought me up some good manure and did some hoeing for me. I planted pansies over by the birch tree so that they may get some shade." She moved her chair over towards the window, as she needed light for her fine work. She then thought of some neighbours and of various small matters that had been on her mind. "I went over to Joseph Arsenault's yesterday. Angie Arsenault helped me with the house cleaning and then she picked some berries for me. Well, Angie is getting married and I took her over a little present."

My father came in and was preparing to wash up in the back room when he stopped suddenly. He had a request to make. "Lizzie," he said, "would you mind coming out to the barn for a few minutes. You might know if there is anything seriously wrong with Old Bob. His mouth seems to be sore. He hasn't been eating too well and I may have to get the vet. I'll get the lantern."

"Yes, of course I'll go," I said. "But I doubt that I will know anything about a horse. If his mouth is sore, what can I do?"

"I thought you might know whether it was really sore or perhaps see something that I missed," he said as we walked to the barn.

The animals had been settled for the night and our going out at that hour disturbed them. They were like people. When the light from the lantern shone into the hen house, the rooster started to crow, thinking it was morning, and Old Bob looked around as if to say, "Well, what is the matter now?" My father tried to peer into his mouth, and I looked, but I could see nothing unusual. I knew nothing about a horse's mouth or even dentistry. Father gave me a quizzical look, and I knew he was wondering about my training. Perhaps he thought we registered nurses were just following the new trend of women going out to work and pretending to know something about medicine.

When we entered the house again, Aunt Mary had lit the largest lamp. Its bright rays fell on the red and white checked cloth. Father would have a good light to read by – that was important to him. Only by reading could he break through the constricting sameness of sowing and reaping, and caring for animals, year after year. Reading brought the outer world to his door and gave him a means of escape into that world.

"Did any mail come for me?" I asked Aunt Mary as she sat in the kitchen. She was darning socks and making neat little patches.

"Yes, some mail came. But Sunday, you had visitors. Some people came to see you, the MacMillans. You nursed Mrs. MacMillan, remember that time Mr. MacMillan came for you? They were in a car, but they came in for a short visit, Mr. and Mrs. MacMillan and four children."

I was sorry to have missed the MacMillans. I wondered how they were? What were the children like now?

Through Aunt Mary's description, I saw a Mrs. MacMillan who was in good health, strong, sturdy, laughing, happy and Mr. MacMillan serious, but a pleasant, genial man. Loretta and Johnny were smart little students, proud of their homework. Rufus, still too young to go to school, had a blue suit with a whistle attached which he wanted to blow while the adults were talking. And the baby was a very pretty, fair child, doll-like blue-eyed and light-haired.

"What did they call the little one?"

"They called her Elizabeth," Aunt Mary smiled proudly.

Calling the child after me was a tribute, but not a special honour as many children in the community were named for the practicing doctor in that vicinity, and some girls were named for the doctor's wife. I wondered how many little Cecilias were running around in honour of Mrs. O'Brien.

As I walked into the kitchen, I noticed a letter addressed to me, postmarked London, England. It would be from Dr. Grant. I tore open the letter and scanned the contents. It seemed he had gone to a large hospital, St. Bartholomew's, and found everything wonderful. It was a nice friendly letter, but I wished that he had said that he missed the hospital, or the nurses, or showed some regret at being away. Instead, he only seemed to rejoice in the size and marvel at the efficiency of the hospital. Well, we were getting along all right without him here. I hoped that when he returned with his added knowledge, he wouldn't be any more exacting or overbearing than he had been previously.

Whether it was the bump on my head or the prying eyes of Aunt Mary, I reasoned that perhaps I needed an escape too. Dr. Grant always wanted me to stay on the Island but had gone away himself. It occurred to me that a change of scenery would do me good. The idea of a large city with its many types of people was fascinating. The Victorian Order of Nurses employed nurses to work in Montreal, and although it would be home nursing which I had been doing in PEI, it would be day duty only, a pleasant prospect. I would merely be exchanging the pastoral setting for the bright lights of the big city. Or so I thought.

Grass and Flowers Should be Somewhere

The sun glinted on the waters of the Strait and shone on the receding shores of the Island. I felt just a little lonely as I leaned against the boat railing, but it was always so when one left home. It was good to be on my way. I would get the train to Montreal in Sackville, and in the morning, I would reach my destination.

"Bil-a-dok, bil-a-dok," came the sound of the wheels on the rails. "Adventure, adventure," they seemed to say. The porter busily made up the berths, and I watched absent-mindedly while thinking of what would await me tomorrow.

In the morning, everybody in the car prepared for their journey's end. Montreal was their destination, and before too long, the buildings stopped flying past the windows, and the train dragged to a stop. All the passengers hurried out, relieved to have this travelling over and to have a chance to walk again in the sunshine.

As I stood at the corner of this great station, the roar

of the city came to me. A young man approached and said, "Taxi, taxi, Mademoiselle, 'otel?"

"Yes, thank you," and I gave my number to him. In a short time, I arrived at the nurse's headquarters.

After a few preliminaries and questions in the office, I was shown to the room that had been assigned to me. I would be together with two other V.O.N. nurses. The head nurse, Mme. Roch-LaPierre, had explained that most of the nurses were at work but would be back for dinner.

Soon after my arrival, a nurse came with me to show me around the city and instruct me in district work. She was very agreeable, and after my instruction period, I missed her company as well as her teaching. Now my biggest problem was to find the streets and the numbers in the maze of the inner city without her help.

My roommates were very kind. Since I was the smallest of the three of us, they called me "La Petite." Because of their sociability, I was never lonely. As we rested on our cots in the evenings, we talked over our experiences – how we managed to find the homes of the sick, how one nurse had taken the wrong streetcar and come back to the starting point, how we struggled with the different languages, and how we were watched by the supervisor, Mme. Roch-LaPierre, who was being especially conscientious to keep an eye on newly arrived nurses that had just started working in the district. We criticized her superior manner and said we'd like to see her take an exam. So long out of training, she probably wouldn't do so well!

Two weeks had passed since I came to Montreal. Riding down St. Catherine Street, I noticed that the motorman called out "Sacatrin," or so it sounded. He called out another name and I heard the clang of metal. The door opened and some workmen with lunch pails, wearing heavy boots, came into the car and began an animated conversation in a foreign language. I decided that they were not quarreling even though they spoke in a loud, excited way. The hour was early, only a few minutes past seven, and many fortunate ones were still in their beds. But the labourers, the housemaids, and all of those who opened up the city were astir. This was their hour. Theirs was the undisputed right to the many vacant seats, and theirs was the right to walk the broad streets unjostled or to the immediate service at the corner stand where they bought tobacco.

"San-Lor-an" sang the conductor nasally. I got off the car and looked about. There was a chubby policeman directing traffic at an intersection. He blew his whistle in a way that reminded me of juvenile performances.

"Where is St. Craig?" I asked.

"Craig Street, it is," he said reprovingly, and gave directions. How different this was from the country atmosphere of Prince Edward Island, I thought as I walked along in search of the number I was given. Could some of these shabby street dwellers be transported, they would consider PEI's fresh fields and streams a wonderfully big park. So much there, so little here. Here, bridges and overpasses were built over roads. There, bridges spanned shimmering water. Here, the high, dark dreary looking buildings were even with the street. Most of them were given over to business, but there were a few rundown dwelling houses. It was summer now, and grass and flowers should be somewhere. However, it seemed that nature had turned a jaundiced eye on this locality.

At some time in the past, some of the dwellings had been built with great ornamentation. Although they were in a dilapidated state, there was much evidence of crenellated wood, many curlicues, and much fretwork on the balconies, windows, and verandahs.

The air was filled with dust and soot and odors not easily identified. I looked up and the smoke drift from a train was going straight up, and I thought, "No breeze today." The hot weather had started early in June, and there was no let up.

I found the number I had been given. If the family could speak no English, I would try a few French words and hope they would understand: "L'eau chaud, l'eau froid, un papier," and at the end, "tout fini." I walked up the steps with an ornamental iron railing on each side and rang the bell. A window opened, and a rather untidy, sleepy-looking head was thrust out. The face was still heavily rouged with, I supposed, last night's makeup.

"What do you want?" the woman started to ask crossly, and then, noticing the uniform, said, "Oh, you'll want Mrs. Staretti. They're on the third floor up."

"Thanks," I said, and climbed up the stairs. Some odors of cooking came to me. That would perhaps be the garlic and spices unfamiliar in Maritime cooking.

I could hear loud talking inside, and when I entered, a stout dark woman, with stockings rolled around her ankles called excitedly, "Joe, Joe, geta up! Da nurse is come here." And to me she said, "Joe, he geta up, and you goa in."

Evidently, the father had no extra bed and shared his wife's bed, even when she was ill or during a confinement. The routine of living was little disturbed by the incident of birth. The home remained the same.

Mr. Steretti came out soon, dressed for work. He must hurry, he said, for the restaurant opened early. He did not seem at all embarrassed, and smiled, showing very good teeth. "Da bambino cute, eh?" He looked quickly at the child in the basket before running down the stairs.

I was thankful that they understood and spoke some English here, and they had sheets and pillowcases. Many of the places where the nurses went had only a feather or straw palliasse under the patient and grey blankets for covering.

In the bedroom, the patient lay back, her dark eyes closed. She would rest all she could for she would have to get up on the fifth day of confinement. Italian women must not be lazy, and her husband would see that she got on her feet, "even if da back ache." Everything that was needed for the bath was brought to her but a comb. Where was a comb? Oh yes, there it was, wrapped up in a piece of paper and put behind the picture of the Virgin with a chubby looking Jesus in her arms.

"Yes, Joe he put dere, so da kids dey not losa!"

Soon the mother was finished, and we smiled at one another in a nice, comfortable way. Now the baby must be bathed.

"Here, we fixa da bambino," the old lady said, bringing

in a dishpan full of warm water, and something else. Some wide strips of flannel to be bound around the child's waist. The swaddle, it was.

"But I can't put that on the baby. The doctor wants the clothing loose so he can kick. We never put swaddling clothes on babies now."

"Maka da back strong. Maka da back strong. Him catcha da cold. Him catcha da cold." The old lady's voice was loud and excited, but her daughter looked on the new ways with more favour. She pointed to a tall, dark cupboard in the room. The grandmother went to the cupboard and finding the clothes, threw them angrily on the bed.

Possibly the grandmother was finding it hard to adjust to the way of life here in the new country, where her eyes looked out on drab, unpainted buildings instead of olive groves and vineyards.

Two little girls came in to look at their baby brother. They had clean faces, but their hair was uncombed, perhaps due to the family comb having been put away.

"See the bambino," said the mother. The younger child's eyes were very round.

"Is it lika da baby Jesus and da Blessed Virgin?"

"No, stupid," said her more sophisticated sister. "The doctor brings the baby. He brought Mrs. LaVerne one, and he brought Mrs. Colletti two, even."

Soon the work was finished, and I was offered a treat by the old grandmother. It was wine and sweet cakes, perhaps given as a peace offering. Then I took my black bag and went out again into the harsh sunlight.

Not Sick at All

There was great activity in the street now that it was almost time for school, and the restaurants and stores were opening up. White-collar workers were hurrying along, many of them looking thin and pale. Soon the brokers of St. James Street, the Wall Street of Canada, would enter the hard, uncompromising buildings of stone and brick and would go about their affairs with their age-old air of knowledge of business and of making money.

But on another street, some untidy children were coming out to play in a small enclosure where some shrubs tried piteously to keep their few remaining branches.

I found the number of the next case quickly enough, but at this house my work would conflict with a religious ceremony. It was the morning of the circumcision. Everything, including the kitchen, bedroom, and dining room was in gala attire. The patient was grand in a pink satin bed jacket with the best sheets and embroidered spread on the bed, and the baby was freshly dressed in a long robe, heavy with embroidery and lace. I could see the long table in the dining room covered with a magnificent lace cloth on which there were many plates of delicacies. All was in readiness for the ancient rite.

No, indeed, there was no work that I could do. "Perhaps you would like a glass of wine, or some little cakes?" the mother offered.

After some quick refreshment, I left and upon finding a telephone in the grocery at the corner, received a new number. When I was through there, I was to go back to headquarters.

The number had to be on the second floor up, and while wandering around looking for an open door for some sign of life, I had the uncomfortable feeling of being observed.

A door opened wide. "Coma here, Nurse. Here plenty sick woman," said a stout man with black eyes set in a pallid face.

The room was dark when I entered, but the man threw open the shutters, and came over to the bedside of a very thin, weak-looking woman who gazed indifferently at the ceiling. Her manner said, "I am not interested in nurses or husbands, or even living."

I looked over the room as I prepared to give a bed bath and general care. There was a marble-topped washstand with basin, a pitcher, a bureau decorated with Plaster of Paris statuary, and above the head of the dark-painted bed, a gold and white crucifix gleamed. A line of clothing stretched from one end of the room to the other. The window faced another large building which blocked a view of the street and partially kept out the air and sunshine.

"You speaka Italiano?" the man asked.

"No, I don't. I am sorry."

"Tu parles français?"

"Je ne parle pas français."

"Well, I knowa what – you Irish!" he exclaimed knowingly.

"What does the doctor think is the matter with your wife?" I countered.

"Well, he not say, but sick, Nurse. Plenty sick here," and he placed his hand in a sorrowful way on a wide expanse of stomach.

"I have no children, but plenty trouble. Are you married, Nurse?"

"No," I replied.

"Well, don't get married – too much trouble. Too mucha."

It seemed that she might have understood some of this conversation, for a stream of Italian erupted at him, and he turned away into the kitchen, muttering, "Too mucha." But he returned with water for the bath, and when I asked about towels, he fussed through the articles on the line until he found some.

A knock came to the door. It was a neighbour with a bowl of broth. Perhaps Mrs. Rossi could take a little. She had put spaghetti in it. The patient moaned and cried out weakly, "Grazie."

"I puta away for later," said Mr. Rossi, taking it into the

kitchen with his smart, quick step.

The patient was propped up on pillows in such a way that she was almost completely clear of the mattress. After bathing and much rubbing with lotion, the pillows had to be replaced one by one. They must be put back in a certain way, and what the patient said in Italian was repeated to me by Mr. Rossi.

"Puta da little one in da small of da back.... puta da biga one under da knee....puta da pinka one here by da arma."

At last, all the pillows had been put in place, the ornaments rearranged, and the picture of the Neapolitan singers tilted at just the right angle so that the patient might have it to gaze on while she took her hot soup which her husband had just brought in. Mrs. Rossi did not seem very grateful, but then she was ill, and patients cannot always be showing their gratitude.

While I was doing the charting, the doctor came in. I had met this man before, and he seemed to be skillful and clever. He was young, Jewish, and very personable.

When the records were completed, I hurried down the stairs and outside. I found the doctor still doing his records in his car. I inquired about Mrs. Rossi's prospects. He said, "There is nothing the matter with her."

"Do you mean that she isn't sick at all?"

"Yes, I mean just that." He shrugged his shoulders. "Oh well, her muscles may have atrophied a little. She has been in bed for ten years. In fact, ever since her child was born. Her baby died, and she never made any effort to get up or help herself since that. She is well physically but has not been able to face reality."

I was taken aback to hear this. All my work and fussing for a woman who wasn't ill.

"Yes." the doctor said, "I told Mr. Rossi, but he wants me to keep coming, and if I didn't attend to her, he would get some other doctor."

After the doctor drove away, I turned my gaze back to the second-floor window and the room where Mrs. Rossi lay in bed. I reconsidered my initial reaction. For after all, was a sickness of the heart not worthy of compassion? Yes, of course it was.

Last Rites

One day, I was assigned cases on Workman Street. This was one of the very poorest of those in the slum district in the vicinity of St. Henry Station. The first number was in the rear of a building, and as I entered over the unpainted threshold, the poverty of the home struck me as forcibly as a north wind. I bathed the patients, mother and baby, and was at the door with my black bag in my hand when the husband came in. He was covered with black grease and grime – face, hands and coveralls, but nevertheless, greeted me warmly with a few words in English. He made me wait, indicating that I must have some appreciation shown me for all the work I had done – at least a glass of beer.

I looked at the unpainted boards of the cupboard where cockroaches came out and ran alone, unmolested along the top shelves, the broken plaster, and the scratched furniture. The cracked and mended window-panes looked out on other poor homes in tenements of the same kind.

The sympathy that welled up within me seemed to have an enervating and deadening effect. I glanced at the wall while he poured the beer. They had a picture, although they had little else – it was the Sacred Heart of Jesus.

The doorway darkened, and looking up quickly, I saw Mme. Roche-LaPierre, the supervisor, who had followed me there. It was her duty to see that the nurses did not neglect their work or take advantage of the fact that they were working on their own. Her eyes were hard, without sympathy, and the lines of her face rigid as she asked, "Haven't you another case yet, Miss MacRae? Hurry, then."

"Yes, of course," I said, flushing, knowing that I looked the picture of guilt, yet resentful because I hadn't wanted the beer. I was only trying to be kind. When my annoyance at myself wore off, I thought how my roommates would laugh over my embarrassment – that I had let myself be caught in such a situation.

The next day, I worked on St. Antoine Street. After the work was finished, I found that I would have to make out a "Free Slip" for the family. There was very little furniture or food and other necessities, and when I asked the necessary questions about income, they didn't seem to understand. Then I went to a different part of the city, but found that I had forgotten some papers, and I had to go back after them. They had been left at the poor home on St. Antoine Street. Stupid of me to forget them, I thought. I would be late getting back to my boarding house where one had better not be too late coming back for the evening meals.

But when I reached the home on St. Antoine Street at

last, I was confronted by a very angry man, the patient's husband.

"Wot business you have ask lotsa ting, eh? Wot business, eh?" He shrugged angrily. And to make the atmosphere still more belligerent, the patient, too, glared at me, she who had been so appreciative earlier in the day. From the man's garbled account, I determined that they had been paid a quick visit by the welfare department.

When I escaped from the harsh atmosphere of St. Antoine Street, I wondered what treatment they had been given by the authorities to have prompted such resentment. But they had learned English so fast! I felt that I was learning fast, too, about the importance of leaving people with their dignity.

Each morning, Mount Royal, with beautiful homes built about its side and nestling at its feet, receded into the distance as we went down to the poorer quarter of the city. At one house, I waited at the door while people seemed to be running up and down stairs and talking excitedly in French – possibly about which door to use. When I heard "porte," I shouted through the door, "Je ne parle pas français." Immediately I heard, "Go roun' de back door. Dis one can't open." At least one person in the house could speak English.

A man met me around the corner of the house. He was a large man with very short arms which he flapped like wings in the excitement of explaining why the front door wouldn't open. A small middle-aged woman met me at the kitchen door. Inside there was a gas stove, a table with chairs, and the unpainted floor was swept clean with everything in order.

"How is it dat you live in Montreal and not speak Français?" she asked me as she took me upstairs to the patient's room. I told her it was difficult, but I was trying to learn.

The patient smiled at me from a bed well-made with white linen, lace trimmed, and nicely ironed. There was much hand work here. I noticed hooked rugs on the floor, and more handmade lace on the bureau scarf and on the looped-back curtains at the little window. There was a small table below the window with candles, a statue of Jesus, and a prayer book. On the walls were brightly coloured pictures of the Saints and the Holy Family.

The middle-aged woman, who was the patient's mother, helped me with the water and towels and then went downstairs to her work in the kitchen. The baby was premature and was bundled up in a nest of absorbent cotton. I thought he should be in an incubator, and when I asked Mrs. Latour, the baby's mother, about it, she said, "I tink de doctor tole me mudder here wot to do. But I tink I get him baptize soon. Maybe tomorrow. No, he don' look awful good, but de doctor, he tink he's all right. I want to name him John Francis."

In a few minutes, the baby's colour had changed still more. The small, yellow face had taken on a deathly pallor. I asked Mrs. Latour's mother about getting a priest, and someone rushed out to the corner phone booth to call his number. The mother, the grandmother, and I kept a sad vigil over the dying baby. Suddenly, realizing that Mrs.

Latour would always remember regretfully that her baby died without baptism, I reached for a bowl of water. How strange I felt, how unqualified to perform any religious rite. Shaking a few drops over the baby's head, I said, "I baptize thee, John Francis Latour, in the name of the Father, and of the Son, and of the Holy Ghost."

Mrs. Latour smiled gratefully at me through her tears, and the grandmother rocked back and forth quietly as we waited for the end. The baby died a few minutes later, and although it had little chance of living, they were very sad. The grandmother hurried to light candles in front of the statue. Many babies did not live through their first week, and the baptizing of babies by nurses was a common thing. They seemed to accept it as a little extra attention thrown in with the bedside nursing.

Most of our patients were maternity cases, but sometimes we had patients who were seriously ill with various diseases. They would die as they had lived, with the noise of a foundry in their ears, with their windows obscured by billowing clouds of smoke, the burning of sulphur in their nostrils, and the dust of a hundred industries in their lungs.

There was no letup in the heat of the summer, and I worked in homes where no breeze came between the crowded buildings. There were many stairs to climb up to the tenement homes and after I had done what I could for the sick at one home, I was off to the next, often enduring long rides on the jolting street cars. I had decided when I came to Montreal that I would do Public Health nursing which would allow me to get to know the city and its people rather quickly, but I had never thought of staying permanently.

Now I wanted to go back to the Island for a rest. I longed for the friendly smiles and the gentle ways of my own people. I was part of them and one who shared their birthright – a daughter of the land!

With these thoughts in mind, I gave in my resignation and packed my trunk with pleasure and expectancy. I was going home.

Flowers for the Cleaning Lady

As I sat in the C.N.R. Station waiting for the Ocean Limited, the train to the Maritimes, I became conscious of a sense of weakness. One of the V.O.N. nurses with a car had offered to help me get my baggage to the railway station, but had brought me early, before she went out to work in the district. The excitement of making the decision to leave Montreal, the packing, and the goodbyes, all kept me from sleeping the previous night, and here I was in an exhausted condition.

I tried to concentrate on the parade of well-dressed people in the rotunda of the station. Even so early in the morning, the French girls always managed to look chic. Now that I was leaving, I wanted to soak it all in for the last time. But things were blurring in front of my eyes. I hoped I wasn't going to be ill. The stifling heat of the summer in the city might have weakened my resistance to germs. I thought that I must have made the right decision to leave the city and go home for a rest.

In a few minutes, my head cleared and I noticed near the newsstand, where people were looking over books and papers, the tall figure of a man somehow seemed familiar. He turned suddenly and spotted me, and my heart thumped when I recognized Dr. Grant! Although I knew he had returned from London, it was a shock to find him here when he was supposed to be on Prince Edward Island. He seemed surprised and pleased to see me and came over to the bench where I was sitting and sat down. "What are you doing here, MacRae? You look as if you were leaving." he said, eyeing my hand baggage. "I just got in last night."

"Yes, I am leaving. I have been doing District work, but I am going home for the rest of the summer. I mind the heat, and I'm tired, too."

His eyes rested on me in a speculative way as he said, "Well, it's a good thing you are going back. I have had quite a few cases where I could have used your help."

"Yes, I might take a case later," I said, "but not just now. I seem to be quite tired out at present." I felt as if the conversation was leading up to something I wasn't quite ready for and didn't want to meet.

He said quietly and thoughtfully, "I did some work on the District myself when I was studying here at McGill. It was hard enough, all right. I had my first case here in Montreal."

"You haven't said how you came to be in Montreal now."

"I just brought a patient up by train to the Royal Victoria

yesterday. I thought the doctors here might have more experience in the rare disease, lupus erythematosus. There is a new drug that they are trying on it. Sulpha, it is called. I just came in here to get a newspaper on my way to the hospital." Changing the subject, "I wrote to you after you left PEI in care of the V.O.N. service, but I didn't get a reply. Did you get my letter? I supposed that you did, as it was never returned."

"Oh, yes, I did get your letter, I am sorry I didn't reply. When you asked me to come back, I was a little confused, and didn't know what to write. I thought it would be best to wait until I returned home to talk to you personally," I said rather lamely. After a pause, he continued, "I am glad to come to Montreal whenever I can. It is good to keep up with new methods and treatments, and the hospitals here are very large and up-to-date. Also, I like to look at different hospitals in case there might be an opportunity for me. They have such a good system for training nurses, too."

"Well, what is wrong with our system?" I asked crossly, my headache and general weakness making my tone rather sharp.

But Dr. Grant went on gently, "Well, for one thing, nurses here are trained to specialize in different branches of medicine such as pediatrics, surgery, etc. They are very professional and never question an order, I have noticed."

I thought miserably, that here is this man, so attractive and knowledgeable, and we can never seem to agree on the essential things! But I put up a weak defense, "I am not sure that I agree entirely. But perhaps, through doing nursing in the country on PEI, one can beome very independent because one has to take care of anything and everything that might arise."

"Well, Elizabeth, it's too early for a serious discussion," he said, and then changing the subject again, "You're not in a hurry to go back to the Island, are you? We could have dinner and see a show, and tomorrow, if my patient is progressing, I think I could go back myself. We could go back together." He peered at me closely, "You have been working too hard, obviously. You are much paler and thinner. Even I, slave driver that I am supposed to be, think that a holiday is coming to you and will do you good. How about staying over for a day? I can get your ticket changed for you." He held out his hand as if with a wave of his hand it would be done!

"Oh no, I must go. They're expecting me at home. I couldn't think of staying, Donald."

Now my mind and my heart seemed to part company, and each took its independent course. I understood now why the ancients might have thought that they were in no way connected. This meeting means nothing to me, said my mind, and my heart went right on being glad. Stay, said my heart, and beat fast at the very thought of it. Dinner and the theatre – a romantic tryst with the handsome, successful doctor!

But I had said that I was unable to stay. My mind was pleased, no doubt. It had its way. It had been victorious. It knew that this overbearing, opinionated medical encyclopedia was not for me.

Your train won't leave for an hour or more. How about going out for a walk? There's a little tearoom on the next street where we can talk. Come, we will check your bag until train time."

Reluctantly, I agreed, and when we left the station and came to the open street, there was a faint breeze and I felt revived. At first my spirits soared, but soon my feeling of extreme fatigue returned. "I think I had better go back now. I don't feel very well," I said, my steps slowing as I shaded my eyes with my hand against the slanted morning rays of the sun.

"Oh yes. We must go back. But there is a nice restaurant here somewhere," he said, grabbing my hand and taking long energetic strides.

I felt as if I were really trailing now as I was being towed along though the increasing crowds of shoppers. Then I began to feel very sick and weak, and very unexpectedly, I began to sob hysterically.

"Don't cry, Elizabeth," the doctor said in a surprised and distressed manner, but I thought he seemed to be giving a command.

"I'll cry if I want to, and you can't stop me," I heard myself saying. Then I felt myself falling dizzily forward. When I came to, I found myself in a taxi. Dr. Grant was supporting my head with one hand, and with the other hand, he was taking my pulse.

I thought at first that it was a dream, or something my subconscious mind had produced because it was too realistic for a dream. Tears were falling on the doctor's light grey suit, and I became embarrassed.

"Somewhere I have a handkerchief. It is very good of you to let me cry all over you like this, but where is my handkerchief?" I fumbled in my purse.

"You can cry all over me any time you want to. Here, take my handkerchief. Now we are at the hospital. Will you be able to walk up the steps, with my assistance, of course?" he said, earnestly solicitous.

"What happened to me? I must have fainted."

"Yes, you fainted on the street, and I decided to get you right to the hospital. I want you to have a complete check-up while you're here," he said as I stumbled up the steps with his arm around me.

When I was admitted to the hospital, a nurse helped me to undress, and then came in to take my temperature.

I said, "Oh, but I don't think I have a temperature," and then I remembered the cardinal rule of hospitals – "Temperatures always to be taken on admission."

"Rest in bed for a few days," was the summation of the resident doctor, "and I think she has a touch of flu."

Dr. Grant left to attend to his own patient, with admonitions for me to stay there and rest completely until he came back.

I had no difficulty in following that order of Dr. Grant's and was asleep almost instantly, only waking to take a little broth at the supper hour. Later I was told that Dr. Grant had been in, but finding me sleeping very soundly, he left again. That explained the flowers that I found on the side table when I awoke early in the morning.

Lying in the bed after the early morning wash given before the night shift nurses went off duty, I listened to the familiar routine of the hospital people scurrying to and fro, muffled orders, the sound of breakfast trays being brought around to the rooms, and the faint aroma of coffee as it was poured into cups. I had slept very soundly and awoke, feeling refreshed. As I ate the breakfast left on my bedside table with a renewed appetite, I realized what I had to do. I must get out of the hospital and make my escape to Prince Edward Island. I had allowed Donald Grant to take over momentarily and make decisions for me, but my sudden illness had intervened and saved me from a path which I felt might destroy me. So now I must go, before I could be committed any further to the earnest doctor's plans for our future.

When the resident came in, I was dressed and determined to convince him that I was not in need of any further hospital treatment. I told him that I had checked my bags at the station for one day only, and I must get there and retrieve them before the train left for the Maritimes. He agreed that I was well enough to leave, and I called a taxi and made my escape, leaving my flowers to the astonished cleaning woman who was scrubbing the floor. I knew that Donald Grant would have no trouble finding someone, perhaps another nurse, who would rejoice in rising with him to the heights of his profession. My future lay elsewhere.

Plain Folks Come Out Ahead

After a week at home, I felt rested and clearheaded. I registered for duty and travelled back to the rooming house in Brighton. I was only in my room for a few minutes when the telephone rang. A man's voice on the wire said urgently and loudly, "Nurse MacRae, can you come to the North American Hotel at once?" Then there was a click. There were no particulars as to who was calling or the nature of the illness. I was hurriedly packing when the telephone rang again, and the same voice said, "Don't take time to walk. Take a taxi, and hurry, please!"

At this second injunction to hurry, I rushed out of the house, forgetting my thermometer and my toothbrush, and ran down the street to the corner garage where a taxi stand was located. I arrived breathless. A car was found and I was whisked to the hotel in a short time. I spoke to the desk clerk, and moments later, I burst into room 160, the number which had been given to me.

There, I found no patient at death's door, and no struggle of any kind was taking place. A doctor was in the room. He introduced me to the patient, a Mr. Horace Mainwaring. The patient looked up at me with worried eyes, and then indicated his very swollen hand. I saw fear in his eyes, but there was also decision and determination. The patient was obviously used to commanding people and expecting them to do his bidding. A desk in the room had a telephone, a stack of papers, and a briefcase upon it. So, it was his voice on the telephone, I realized, thinking of the urgency in it.

The doctor produced a sterile scalpel, and I arranged towels and dressings. Swiftly and mercilessly, an incision was made, and at once blood and fluid gushed out. The doctor applied disinfectant and dressings.

Mr. Mainwaring spoke again in a happy voice, "The pain is almost gone! You did fine, Doc. Here, how much do I owe you?" With one hand, he worked out some bills from his bulging wallet and negotiations were completed.

"Yes, you should be all right now. Give him these tablets, Nurse, and apply a hot boracic dressing. I will see him tomorrow." Turning to the patient again, he said, "You should get Miss MacRae to come every day and change the dressings."

When the doctor left, the patient chatted as if it relieved his feelings to talk. "And to think I worried so much about the finger, Nurse. You know, I should have had this attended to before now, but I dreaded it."

He explained that he had come to the Island from

Toronto to look at a business proposition but had found the roads difficult to travel during the spring break-up, and the trains were very slow between Charlottetown and other parts of the Island.

During the summer, his hand had become infected. A wave of self-pity overtook him, and he began in a complaining tone, "My wife is in New York now on a visit. I sent her a wire saying that I was sick and would have to stay here for a while, but I haven't heard from her. I guess she is too busy having a good time! And is she hard to please! Most women are like that, hard to please. I give her a lot of money to spend, but is she grateful? No, she is not."

Before I left, he asked me to return each day as the doctor requested. He seemed to expect that I would accept the work without question. Mentally, I calculated that I might have to work a late or midnight shift in order to be free to do an hour's work for him, but as if reading my mind, he offered to pay me for a half day's work if I would come.

The following day he was again talkative. "You ought to come to Toronto. The big hospitals there are beautiful, and you would be well paid."

I thought to myself that the "big-city" people seemed to measure everything in terms of money. How much you earned, and how much things cost, and where you could get the best for your money – these things were of so much more importance than the colour of maples, or the health of a neighbour, or the personalities of the animals in one's care.

He continued to complain daily about his wife. "I built a lovely home for her in Toronto and a summer cottage at Lake Couchiching, but is she happy? No, she is always complaining about something."

"Well, what about husbands?" I asked. "Aren't they hard to please?"

"That depends on whom you get. Not all men are hard to please," he said, smiling. "You never married, did you?" I shook my head, and he looked at me speculatively, as if to discover what dreadful secret I was hiding.

I heard so much about his wife being selfish, extravagant, and disagreeable, that in my mind, this unknown woman appeared to be the cause of all marital unhappiness. Then one day while he was talking about his wife, he broke down and wept. I didn't know what to say because I was no marriage counsellor. It was enough to look after a wounded finger and much easier to cure than a wounded heart. I was wondering how I could tell him that his finger was sufficiently better that he did not need me any longer. I was applying a dry dressing when I heard a swish of feminine clothing and got a sniff of some expensive perfume. A large but rather pretty woman of indefinite age swept past me, rushed to Mr. Mainwaring and threw her arms around him.

"You dear boy! Here alone and sick!" she exclaimed. "I came as soon as I could leave my poor dear Auntie Mary. Is your finger better?" She kissed him, and I looked to see his reaction to all of this. It was written all over him – delight and satisfaction.

"Miss MacRae, this is my wife," he said fatuously with shining eyes and holding her hands in both of his. "She just came in on the train from New York. It's wonderful to see her."

She looked at me thoughtfully, then smiled and I smiled back. It was just as well that Mrs. Mainwaring would never know that she had been cruelly criticized and condemned. Perhaps they had had a quarrel, and the illness had softened the wife's heart so that all was forgiven and forgotten, I reasoned.

Mr. Mainwaring paid me and thanked me, but I knew he cared little how soon I left, for now he had Dorrie, his wife. She bustled around getting food from the kitchen and getting a book that "Horrie" had been reading and wishing to finish, telling him about something that had happened in New York. Dorrie insisted that she would do the dressings herself and suddenly took on the stature of a Florence Nightingale.

I left feeling somewhat deflated, and yet a little relieved to think that my presence might have stirred some wifely jealousy. Perhaps Dorrie would be jolted out of her complacency to appreciate her husband and all that he provided.

At the registry office, finding that there were many nurses ahead of me waiting for work, I went home for the weekend. Here everything seemed as usual, with my aunt bustling around, my father quiet and tired, and Uly glad to see me. He asked about Leoda Mooney and I told him that the doctor said her condition was serious and her chances of recovery slight. I had visited Ida May at the orphanage and had found her happy and playing with other children.

That night, I went to my quiet little room, a soft bed, and everything favourable to sleep. No rumbling of cars and wagons, no trains thundering and whistling; the world seemed to have stopped for sleep.

About six a.m., I was awakened by a loud, urgent thumping on the outside door. I waited, holding my breath, but the thumping continued until Uly went down to the door. It was as I feared, an emergency case brought on by a kidney ailment. I was totally unprepared, with no uniform at home and no suitcase of "accoutrements" like Mr. O'Brien. But I must go. I vowed I wouldn't be caught like this again. I would be prepared for any emergency from now on.

Aunt Mary was up and wanted to help. "There is an old uniform of your Aunt Louisa's in the attic. I can get it if you wish," she offered.

I shuddered when I thought of Aunt Louisa's uniform. Aunt Louisa had worn it before she went to do missionary work in the South Pacific, and she had been a tall willowy woman. But I supposed I must accept it.

"Here it is. Will it do for you, do you think?" My aunt said this hesitatingly as she came in with a yellowed, wrinkled uniform. "I'll just have to pin it where it is too big."

I fussed with the old-fashioned garment and resorted to safety pins at intervals, then quickly got into the waiting car and was on my way to the home of John and Annie Maud Barnes. When I arrived with the neighbour who brought me, a worried-looking woman introduced herself as Annie Maud. She said the doctor, who had just left, had ordered an ice cap and pills. The doctor was from Summerside – a Dr. Barkham.

Annie Maud was a big woman, dressed in tight blue overalls which bulged uncomfortably in many places, men's wool socks, and a tattered straw hat. I assumed at first that she was so concerned with the sick man that she had neglected her own appearance. I found out later that Annie Maud had been up all night watching over her husband and now was dressed to go out to do the chores. There was a good wood supply in the kitchen, chopped ice, which she had obtained from a neighbour's icehouse, and ice-cold water from the pump in a pitcher by her husband's bedside.

The light of the morning was flooding the room when Mr. Barnes opened his eyes and looked at me with doubt and perplexity. "He is better, isn't he?" Annie Maud said, and brought the medicine which the doctor had left. This was not the first sickness of this kind that John Barnes had had, and Annie Maud knew what should be done.

Now that the emergency was over, I thought of how I must have looked when I arrived with my uniform hanging grotesquely about me. Annie Maud had already been out in the barn that morning and hadn't bothered to change out of her work clothes. Her tight overalls on her rounded figure and her short thin hair made her look like Humpty Dumpty. We are an odd-looking pair, I thought. As Annie Maud went back and forth between her stove and the back bedroom where the sick man lay, I noted a slight odor from the stables which mingled with the antiseptic smell of the sick room, and the contrast between her and "Dorrie" Mainwaring struck me forcibly! Annie Maud was doing everything in her power to help me and to care for her husband with no thought of herself, and my heart warmed to her.

The next day, John was strong enough to be propped up in bed. He talked about his health and his medicine until I decided he thought about his symptoms too much. He also seemed to have a decidedly childish faith in pills and potions.

"Dr. Barkham said I had a 'vunclir' disease and he gave me that medicine in the bottle, there. Smell it, Nurse. You may be able to tell what it is." He pushed a bottle of greenish liquid up to my nose.

"No, I don't believe I can tell, but if it helped you..."

"He charged me $7.50 for it, so it ought to be all right. I was terrible sick with backache last winter, so I tried Morton's Kidney and Liver pills. I don't think my liver and gallbladder was right. Annie Maud had to nurse me for a month," he said, rolling his eyes to the ceiling.

I wondered briefly if I would earn my pay for listening as much as for nursing on this case.

"Oh, he ain't so bad now," said Annie Maud cheerfully as she sat down at noon to eat a hurried dinner, "but one swallow don't make a summer." Her farm work gave her little time to visit, but her devotion to John was steady and unwavering.

I looked closer at my patient. The chronically ill are often enveloped in a cocoon of anonymity, impenetrable and unrevealing as to their personality. Now John Barnes was emerging as a definite character with a morbid interest in symptoms and disease. Perhaps only a psychiatrist could probe his subconscious and find the trouble.

"I had awful trouble with shaky hands," John went on, his voice becoming stronger as he warmed to the topic, "and I had a funny feeling in my tongue. I told the doctor about it and he didn't seem to know what it was. That was Dr. White that didn't know, so I went to Dr. Barkham and he gave me a bottle of medicine. I think it's time for my pink pill now, and you can give me Barkham's green medicine, too."

I measured out the dose prescribed, and as there was little else to do, I looked for a book to read. From a bookcase, I found an old book, *Domestic Recipes* by R. Moore. Besides the recipes, there were cures for many diseases. I read one out to Annie Maud about a cure for lockjaw which said it would be very effective to rub turpentine into a wound. I'm afraid I hooted a bit in derision and my scorn struck a sour note.

"Well, I don't know. They say turpentine is very good for a lot of things," Annie Maud said, and by her manner I thought she was a little on the defensive.

"Yes, turpentine is good," John spoke up from his bed. "Once I stepped on a nail and I put turpentine on it, and it was well in no time."

"But they give anti-tetanus serum now if they think there is danger of lockjaw," I said. "In fact, it is best to go and have a dose of it if the wound is deep and if there has been dirt near it."

I read with interest the section on nursing. It ordained that a nurse should be selected with care. A woman of intelligence, kind and amiable with good manners and an even temper should be procured if possible. I wondered if I would pass these requirements or even come close.

Dr. Barkham came that afternoon. He was tall and very fair, his youthfulness accentuated by the band of freckles across his nose. Are they graduating them younger, I wondered, or am I getting old?

"Have you a chart?" he asked, when he understood that I was a nurse. "I see you have been able to take a little milk," he said to John as he looked at my notes. "Now let me see your tongue, please."

When the doctor had finished examining him, John said, "I've been meaning to tell you Doctor, I get the worst sensation in my hands. What could be the cause of that?"

"A nervous condition, I imagine, but it should clear up when you grow stronger. When you are able to get outdoors in the sun, you're bound to feel better."

"I hope you're right, Doctor. And I have pains in my legs and arms."

"I'll give you a bottle of medicine for that, Mr. Barnes, and I'll send out some pills for your nerves. The kidney condition is clearing up, but all those vague pains and sensations are a different matter."

When he was leaving, he confided to me, "He is suffering from hypochondria as well, and that isn't easily cured."

When the doctor had gone, Annie Maud told me of

how she worked when her husband had taken ill some years before. "At first, when John took sick, I had to work very hard to make a living for us, because the place was mortgaged and John wasn't able to work. He ain't able to work much yet, but we ain't so poor now. It was as if something said to me, "If you don't work hard, you will starve and freeze to death, so I worked with all my strength. I put up a good fight with help only at cropping and harvest. I cared for John and worked in the fields, too. I even cut down little hardwood trees in the woods and dragged them home to cut for firewood. Sometimes I would be so tired and discouraged, I would cry, and one evening I fell asleep by the pile of sticks, too done out to go on. In the morning, first thing I heard was John calling me. He had a bad scare – thought I died, I guess. But I won out in the fight against poverty. I was able to pay off the mortgage, so now what I make is our own."

"But I began to look a fright. My skin got hard and wrinkled, being out in the sun so much, and the harder I worked, the fatter I got. When I drove the truck wagon into town people stared and the children laughed. 'There's that funny Mrs. Barnes coming,' they'd say. They couldn't know what my life was like. But I'm going to go and get fixed up. I'll get a permanent at the beauty parlour one of these days."

I said nothing. What was there to say? We sat in companionable silence as we waited for the car which would take me back to my home. Now that the patient greatly improved and Annie Maud had somebody doing the work in the barns, I could leave.

Before I left, I gave John a dose of the new medicine. It was pink and could have been a tonic that would stimulate the patient's appetite. But as he looked at me with child-like expectancy in his eyes, I knew he saw it as something with magical powers to relieve all his aches and pains that were so distressingly real to him.

The neighbour who had brought me came to drive me home, and Annie Maud stood at the door to see me off. I realized that here was a truly happy woman who would always be a good friend, somebody who could be counted on. I wondered if she went to a beauty parlour and then bought herself new clothes, would her personality change too? I decided that I liked her as she was.

Third Day "Blues"

The third day of disease has always been an important and prognostic day in the medical profession. The third day after an operation or a delivery has been important enough to demand a visit from the doctor, if at all possible. If bacteria are found in the blood on that day, there might be incipient signs of illness, a headache, or a temperature.

The third day after the birth of Gillis' son began almost joyfully. The sun streamed into the pretty upstairs bedroom, and Gillis felt physically well and quite elated over the little bundle of perfection in the basket. I was pleased that she had asked me to take her case, and being with her reminded me of our training days together. Dr. MacLeod was in charge, which easily brought us back to former times. We had always liked Dr. MacLeod.

"Don't you think he is prettier than the babies we nursed in the hospital?" Gillis asked. From the vantage point of maternity, she felt a tenderness towards all babies, but this one in particular seemed especially good and beautiful.

"Yes, he is a lovely baby, and I love him because he is your child," I said as I busied myself preparing his bath. "Now, which clothes do you wish him to wear today, the blue jacket and the booties that his auntie made for him?"

The baby's father, Stanley, then came in to gaze adoringly at the miniature of himself. It was his lunch hour, but it was becoming his custom to come home just to involve himself in the conversation about the baby's bath, the baby's clothing, or the baby's drinking water – all topics of considerable importance and cause for fatherly solicitude.

Dr. MacLeod came in, his eyes beaming with happiness and contentment. "You're fine," he said to Gillis, "and the baby is good. He is sleeping well and he's an excellent colour." He peered into the basket. "I'll see you tomorrow."

Some of Gillis' friends had stopped in with more blue outfits and would return when she was feeling stronger. Some of our former classmates from the hospital had telephoned to offer help – but it was with the housekeeping that we could have used some assistance. The housemaid was very young and inexperienced. She could manage the kitchen range and cook substantial meals, but she did not understand how to operate the wood and coal furnace very well and had put too much coal in it just before noon, for a day that grew unseasonably warm in the early afternoon.

"Did you put more coal on, Cecile?" I asked, but she did not understand if we wanted more heat or less heat until she saw me opening all the doors and windows. Then she helped me to close all the heating vents and shut the draft on the furnace, sincerely contrite.

I took Gillis' temperature and found it quite high, and she complained of a headache and discomfort. Finally, she began to cry, no doubt thinking of the possibility of infection starting on the third day. Her anxiety might be the result of the patient being a nurse and knowing too much of what could happen, I thought.

I telephoned the doctor, but he did not seem too alarmed. He had seen her three hours earlier. Usually, his patients recovered quickly and he boasted that he had never lost an obstetric patient or had a case of "purple fever," as they called the infection, otherwise known as puerperal fever. To pacify me, he gave me a prescription to be filled at the drug store and said he would call in the morning. The day that had started out so well had turned into a "blue" day after all.

But that evening, Gillis felt much better. She had taken the medicine and her temperature had come down with the temperature of the house. It seemed that she had weathered the crisis. The baby lay beside her on the bed, his blond hair brushed up to a little peak, his blue eyes looking at nothing in particular. Just looking at him brought a surge of happiness.

"I can't decide who he looks like. Sometimes I think he looks like Stanley and sometimes like Mother, but sometimes when he screws up his face, I think he looks like Aunt Sophia Bell," Gillis declared, laughing.

The next morning, her mother came for a visit; she was

flushed with excitement and happiness. Again, the subject of whom the baby resembled was discussed.

"He looks like you did, Isabel, when you were a baby," she said. "Yes, I would know him anywhere and know he belongs to our family." This was pronounced in decisive tones, disregarding the fact that the child bore Stanley's name, and had Stanley's family characteristics as well.

"Yes, he does look like both our families," said Gillis quickly. "So we thought we would call him William Alexander, after his two grandfathers."

"William Alexander! Yes, those are two good names." She nodded approvingly. "And is he good at night, Isabel?"

"Yes, he doesn't fuss at night at all," Gillis said with pride.

"You won't get up before the tenth day, will you, Isabel?" Mrs. Gillis asked, looking anxiously at her daughter.

"Well, whatever the doctor says," Gillis replied cautiously.

"Yes, of course. You do just as he says. Sadie Sadler got up the ninth day and she had to go right back to bed. She was awful sick. Don't you remember her, Isabel?"

'Yes, I suppose she had a relapse," Gillis said as she raised herself up on her elbow, and in a teasing voice said, "I really feel strong enough to get up right now."

"Oh, but this is a false feeling of strength. Do be careful! I think it is wise to be cautious, don't you, Elizabeth?" She looked at me for support.

"Yes," I agreed. I happened to have my book, *Private Duty Nursing* open at "Confinement," and I read in part:

"The patient should return to her household as a rested, well woman, and she cannot unless she has taken proper time to recuperate. The patient may be physically able to be out of bed and on her feet at the end of ten days, and to go downstairs at the end of two weeks; but as soon as she leaves her room, the responsibilities of the house rest upon her and the nurse can no longer shield her from over-fatigue, from too much company, or from household perplexities."

Mrs. Gillis had been thinking along those lines, and she nodded gravely as I read. In fact, everything from that point on met with her approval. She watched while I changed the baby and put him to the breast. She beamed with satisfaction when she saw that he nursed well. It was a very happy day for all concerned.

That night, I shared my bedroom with Mrs. Gillis, and when we were preparing for sleep, she spoke of the thought uppermost on her mind. When she had put on a mauve gown and had taken out her teeth, she said, speaking in a slurred tone without her upper plate, "God has been good to Isabel. She has such a good husband, a lovely baby, and a nice home. Now you'd wonder why one girl would be so fortunate, wouldn't you?"

I looked down at my shapeless blue flannel bathrobe which the sales clerk had assured me would be warm for night work, and my beaded leather slippers which already looked a little scuffed about the toes. I nodded in agreement, but my train of thought was suddenly jolted in an odd direction. Had I been neglected in some way? Empty arms, and to all appearances an empty heart?

Mrs. Gillis settled down immediately to sleep, all her worries about her daughter's state of health having been assuaged.

I turned my face to the wall on my side of the bed and reflected on the possible causes of my still unmarried state. I had to admit that I had succeeded thus far in avoiding anything more than casual meetings with the stout bachelor farmers of whom Father and Aunt Mary spoke so highly. Had the hardships and poverty in some cases that I had seen in country homes frightened me of marriage? On the other hand, I reasoned that the alternative possibility, becoming the wife of a successful doctor, would be far from a life of poverty, at least in the material sense. But there was also poverty of spirit, an unbearable thought. I had closed the door to any further thoughts of Donald Grant. I would choose a quieter, gentler path forward.

Samson Among the Foxes

On the Labour Day weekend, Martin and I managed to get away to her home at Bedeque.

"Do you think we should pour whites of eggs down his throat?" asked Martin anxiously as we looked down at a struggling dog. Bill Martin had brought us his dog, Reddy, carrying him in his arms while he twitched and shook with a convulsion – the term applied to the lower animals when they were stricken. The dog was a small foxhound, and Bill had just found him lying under a tree, violently ill. I hoped we could do something for him. The veterinarian was away, and even if he were home, his cases were mostly of farm animals.

Whites of eggs? But whites of eggs were given after a poison, a caustic poison, so as to lessen the burning effect on the mucus membrane. Bill could not believe that anyone would have left poison around. Where would he have found it?

We found some old coats and made a bed for the dog behind the kitchen stove. Perhaps if he were warm, the dreadful twitching would stop. However, the twitching continued. What could we do?

A warm bath was usually given to a child with convulsions, to relax the muscles. It was an old remedy. We would try it. The next step was to get the wash tub with a supply of warm water. The dog did not mind our attention, perhaps only partly aware of what was going on. I knelt on my knees and immersed the dog. Bill's brother, George, came in to watch and disapproved of the bathing. "If the dog dies, Bill will never forgive you for washing him," he said as he stood and watched.

"What do you think of giving him an enema?" I asked Martin.

Willing to try anything, we gave the enema, but through everything the twitching continued. I tried the dog's pulse, feeling at the paw for where I considered the radial artery would be. The pulse was very weak. I would administer a stimulant for the heart. We boiled the needle and gave the hypo.

Bill came in to look at his pet with his anxiety evident in his serious expression. There was nothing more we could do, unless we tried the whites of eggs. We did this and the dog vomited. "We should have given the whites of eggs in the first place," his sister said.

We sat and waited as we would have watched by the bedside of a very ill patient. Some hours later the twitching stopped, but so did the weak little heartbeat. Tears came to my eyes. I had not helped at all. I had treated the dog as I would treat a child, but my efforts were unsuccessful. Bill noticed my distress and turned to console me. It was good of him to consider my feelings while he was suffering the loss of a well-loved pet.

Sometime later, the weekly paper reported that Bill Martin had lost a valuable foxhound. Bill noticed it and said, "There was a nice obituary in the paper today about Reddy." He read it out, and then continued solemnly, but with a suspicious twinkle in his eye, "And in the eulogy, the minister compared him to Samson among the foxes." Bill's mother reproved him for speaking so lightly of a Biblical story. Mrs. Martin was a serious-minded woman who had been a schoolteacher in her youth. She was intellectual and read the classics, but she usually enjoyed the levity of her children, who were all endowed with a Dickens-like sense of humour which I found delightful. Although my introduction to the family had been through Martin, my attachment to Bill was now growing.

Martin rose to put more wood on the fire. The sun streamed in from the two windows. It was cheerful and comfortable here in the warm living room.

"Isn't it strange that people worry so much about things that don't matter. How they will do their work, what they will eat, how they will dress, how they will act on certain occasions, what flowers they will put in their hooked rugs, when nothing matters but life and death."

"Yes, that is so true," I agreed. We had both been in the throes of poverty and sickness. We had watched by too many bedsides, where we hoped that life might be spared, to think that social amenities were all-important.

There was a tap on the door, and Martin rose to answer it. An Indian woman came in with Martin. Her dark face was bright with happiness. She had come bearing gifts: a large paper bag full of cranberries and a newspaper-wrapped parcel of smelts.

"Here," she said "I brought you this. For kindness to me when I be sick. You help me. You good to me. I try to be good to you." She smiled at Martin as she pushed back a piece of cotton on her forehead which she had tied around her straight, black hair.

"I bring pretty little basket for you too."

Martin smiled, thanked her and took her gifts out to the kitchen while the woman seated herself by the fire. "Chilly," she said and shivered a bit. Her clothing was not warm enough for this fall day. A light summer coat covered a cotton dress.

"Did you hear 'bout my brother?" she asked Martin when she returned. "Well, not my brother 'zactly, his wife. She take the stroke, you know. She die first on one side, then the other. She not get better. They live on reservation," she said and for a minute looked sad, but brightened and told of happenings at the camp which was quite near to Martin's home.

We sat and listened. This was a happy event. The gratitude of a patient was one of the rewards of nursing. The weariness caused by lack of sleep, the worry, the blame, the fact that we were often shut in with uncongenial people, the lack of social life, became a half-forgotten memory. Now, we laughed and talked. Nursing was good. We didn't have a care in the world.

Martin busied herself with cutting flannelette for diapers. She was hemming for an expectant neighbour and the Indian woman looked at Martin and the diapers with suspicion. Martin explained that a busy mother had asked for her help. Now the woman seemed relieved. "Oh, I thought for yourself," and then she confided her troubles. We were good listeners.

"We not want our Mary to go over to Island but she go and there she catch baby. We not want her to go," she said sadly.

"You have any bright-coloured paper?" she asked. "I make flowers. I sell some, but only lonesome colours left."

We wondered what a lonesome colour would be. Martin showed her some colours and it seemed that the colour she described was mauve. Perhaps she was right; it was used in funerals. Martin found some bright coloured tissue which seemed to greatly please her. Also, she found a warm winter coat and woolen scarf, so that when the visitor rose to leave, she was prepared for cold winds and wintry storms in the coming months.

We watched her leave. She had put the coat over the thin, summer wrap and had tied up her head in the warm scarf.

"What was the matter with the woman? What was her illness?" I asked Martin.

"It was the flu. She had a high temperature, and in the

tent, it was hard to give nursing care. I did what I could to make her comfortable and brought her food. Fortunately, she was sick only a short time. But she was grateful as you can see." I tried to think what it would be like to be ill and lie in a tent. It was too hard to comprehend. I gave up trying to imagine the discomfort.

"What do they eat, anyway?" I asked.

"They hunt ducks and geese and get fish from the river. They pick berries when they are in season for their own use and to sell in town. They also make baskets, axe handles, nets for fishing and sometimes chair seats and tables. I must take you over to the camp. There are not so many camping now as some have gone to the reservation, Lennox Island.

The following day was warm and sunny. It was a perfect day for a walk. We had only to cross the main road, take a walk through a spruce wood and come to an open field, the Indian camping ground. Only two tents were here in the field surrounded on three sides by a wooded area. Some trees of spruce, maple, poplar and pine bordered the river, which was a tidal river, near the sea. I thought at once of Evangeline. "This is for forest primeval, the murmuring lines and the hemlocks." I could understand that in the summer, at least, the Indians would be loath to leave this spot.

The expectant mother, for whom Martin had cut the flannelette, sat at the open tent. She was busy with strips of wood cut paper-thin which she was weaving with infinite skill and patience into a pretty basket. She had coloured the wood with dye, some of which was made from plants and bark of trees. Her face lit up with a pleased expression when she saw Martin. But a sad look came to her dark eyes as she continued weaving the strips of wood. Her straight, black hair fell over her face as she looked at her work. She said nothing.

Martin asked her how she was feeling, and she smiled and said, "All right." But I felt that all was not right, as Martin had told me her community could be very severe with one who strayed from the beaten path.

That evening, at home with the Martins, when we were laughing over humorous incidents that Bill was telling, a man came looking for a nurse for his wife who was feeling unwell. As Martin had signed up for a maternity case, I couldn't refuse, although I wished that I could remain in this setting of carefree happiness. Regretfully, I packed my bags and went with him. But not before Bill extracted a promise from me to return as soon as possible.

Scotch Cakes and Cherry Wine

A cool wind caught me as I stood on the Hunter River Station platform. Time had passed. October was not far off. The seasons came and passed quietly, very often unnoticed, and now another winter was coming.

Hunter River had been called after a Mr. Hunter who had lost his way in a wintry storm and had perished. The story was sad and perhaps, in a sentimental way, that was why his name was perpetuated for all time. He had returned from the war of 1812-14 in Upper Canada to find his sweetheart, whom he had hoped to marry, already married to another. This had been too much. In shock and sorrow, he had wandered out in a stormy night and had been overcome.

But today, Hunter River did not mirror Mr. Hunter's unhappiness. It reflected only the light and sunshine of a September day – the painted houses along its banks with brightly coloured roofs, the light and darker green of the trees with a few already turning colour were mirrored in a placid surface. From a short distance came the continuous, gurgling sound of water flowing from a mill.

Uly had come to meet me in a car. I had been used to a wagon with Old Bob, but times had changed. Horses and buggies were becoming fewer. Uly looked a bit thinner. He seemed changed too. There was a thoughtful expression in his eyes that I had never noticed before. He had grown up, but I was unprepared for the plans he had made.

"I am planning on going back to school – to college. I would like to be a doctor, if I ever could be. I know I will have to work hard."

"That would be wonderful."

"You know, I noticed at the ploughing matches, at the races, at threshing, somebody could always beat me, but at school I always came first in my class."

This was a splendid idea, but how could it be arranged? Uly was the only son. There was the farm to care for, continuous work. I believed this about his studies; he had been bright in school.

I should not have underestimated Uly, for he had everything planned. Part of the farm was already rented, and Father had a liking for carpentering on which he had been spending more and more time. Some lumber was to be sold for the expense of college, then teaching for a time as many had done before entering university. As he spoke, I believed it could be done, Uly a doctor. How good it would be.

In the yard, my father came to the car to meet us. He

looked well. He was cheerful, asking about my work and how long I would be home to visit.

Aunt Mary was bustling around getting dinner. "We have chicken," she said, "and I made an apple pie." Her attitude toward me had changed. I had continued nursing and she had heard nothing against me from her neighbours. Public opinion was the yardstick by which one could be accepted or rejected. And everyone was subjected to its chameleon-like change.

In the living room, I was glad to see that the stuffed owl with his large, green, glass eyes had gone. But Aunt Mary refused to part with the picture of Queen Victoria, although she was long dead. She was a fixture, supporting, unchanging, giving stability, so she hung in prim certitude, at variance with our new chesterfield and chintz-covered chairs.

Our noon dinner over, I walked out to an adjoining field. The grain had been cut, and the sun shone brightly on the yellow stubble. From a distance came the roar of the ocean, the eternal, continuous beating of the waves on the shore. Looking north, one could see some deeper blue of water and an outline of the French convent. Some birds flew overhead; perhaps with some not understandable intelligence, they were preparing for a journey south. Some crickets chirped, a brown caterpillar, with a seemingly definite destination, crossed my path. I picked a tiny wildflower, too small to be noticed, but perfect in exquisite colouring and markings. Here the cruelty of nature was carefully hidden. The flying birds, the chirping and movement of the insects, the warm sunshine, all seemed to destroy the idea of pain and death.

The red road beyond the field looked inviting. I decided to call on Anselm and his wife. I had been told about the place he had recently bought, a white house with a bay window, not more than a mile away. I recognized the bay window at once. The pleasing sight of white frilled curtains came to me from freshly washed panes.

The door opened at once. There in truth was Mrs. Sheeham, now Mrs. Richardson. "Come in, Nurse," she said at once, taking my hand, "I often wondered if I would ever see you again. And one day I was thinkin' of when we last met, and I wondered if we might meet some day in Heaven. You're tired after walkin'! I'll make some tea."

She set about the earthly task of making tea, holding the teapot away from her spotless dress and shaking it vigorously. "To stir up the leaves, you know. I made some scotch cakes this morning, an' I made some cherry wine, too. I'll get a bottle."

"How have you been feeling, Mrs. Richardson?"

"Fine, you know I took some of that medicine that poor Matilda told us about. You know, the picture on the bottle of the man jumpin' in the air, the bitters. It's awful good medicine."

As she talked, I looked about the room which, clean and orderly, decidedly reflected Mrs. Richardson's taste in decoration. Small plastic birds were attached to the frilly window curtains, also a string of birds continued along the adjoining wall, below the picture of Sir William Wallace.

Mrs. Richardson came forward with the wine. She was wearing a rose dress, unusually short for her. I guessed the dress was one of her trousseau. At any rate, it had a suggestion of youth; it brought colour to her face so that there was a transformation. Although some time had passed since I had seen her at Matilda Richardson's, she looked years younger. She laughed as she helped herself to more cherry wine.

Anselm came in. He had always been cheerful. His eyes had always twinkled even when there was little comfort or cheer. Now there were no complaints, no orders, no definite schedule thought out by Miss Matilda. Now he was a free man and definitely happier.

"I bought this place, Miss MacRae. I liked it out here, and after poor Matilda passed away, I was lonely. Even Adrian left."

"Where did Adrian go?"

He bought a small farm. Matilda left him some money, and then with the wages he had saved, he was able to buy the farm and buy some machinery, enough to start. He is married now. I was over to see him and his wife the other evening. He is a good worker and his wife seems to be a smart little woman."

"I have rented the land that came with this place. Now, I just cut the grass and tend to the flowers. I am planning to plant an orchard at the back there. To have one's own apples and cherries and plums, it is good."

"Yes, and a crab apple tree, so I can make jelly; the juice of them little apples jells so well." Mrs. Richardson's eyes became dreamy.

I admired the bouquet of flowers on the brightly varnished table. There was a large, black japanned box near the flowers.

"That's my ammunisha box," Mrs. Richardson said when we had admired the flowers. "Joseph, my first husband, liked to go shootin' ducks down on the marsh. He'd rather go shootin' than anythin' else, so I always had to get ammunisha for him when I went to town. I kept the box, the only thing I had left to remind me of him."

I looked at Anselm, but his eyes only twinkled. He did not mind the ammunition box.

I was invited to stay for supper, but I had in mind another call. I said goodbye, and they waved to me as I started down the road. The happiness of these two congenial people stayed with me. I hoped my next visit would be as pleasant. Often, I had noticed, one only knew so much happiness, as if it were measured. Nature wished to keep spirits on an even tenor so that joy was very often followed by sadness.

A Bird of Bright Plumage

I became aware of a regular noise of horse's hooves behind me. I stood aside as a young man in his early teens in a horse and wagon came up. "Miss," he said as he gave a strong pull at the reins.

I knew him slightly, Billy Baxter, from the California Road. I was getting a bit weary, so I climbed in beside him. "Thanks," I said. "You were very good to stop for me."

"Yes," he agreed. "I never pass anyone on the road. I always ask them if they'll take a lift," he continued in curious self-approbation. "How do you like this nursin' business?"

"Very well. Sometimes it is hard."

"Yes, I guess so, I imagine."

Then, turning to me with clear, curious eyes he asked, "Could you tell me what is good for warts? I have one and it kinda bothers me. It's on me right hand. They say if you take a piece of raw meat and rub it on the wart, then bury the meat the wart will go; when the meat is rotting away the wart goes. That's reasonable."

"I don't think that is reasonable. If you have nitric acid, you can burn it off gradually; just a bit on the end of a match every day, but one has to be careful with acid, you know. It eats away almost anything. Now, I am not too sure you can get nitric acid without a prescription..."

"Oh, I know all about acids and the likes," he said confidently as he tapped the horse with a long stick he carried for a whip. He pulled the reins again, but neither the stick nor the jerking reins made any impression on the horse. He did not increase his slow gait. In a steady rhythm, he could almost be keeping time to music.

"What is good for the pain from the sting of wasps? I ran into a nest when we was threshin'. They sting somethin' awful."

"Yes, I know. I think the pain is caused by an acid in the sting. I think baking soda or anything alkaline would help."

"I put some clay on the sting and it seemed to help," he leaned forward, tapped with his stick, pulled at the reins and looked up at Mr. MacLeod, the minister, who was just walking out of a driveway, preparing to get in his car. The minister smiled and waved and Billy said, "How do you do, Mr. Macleod." Then leaning forward again he tapped and jerked the reins. Thinking of other ailments, he went on, telling of a sore tooth, a sore back and a sore shoulder. "After we finished threshing, I had an awful pain in me' shoulder, I had to go to the doctor. He said it was broositis or somethin'. He gave me somethin' to put on it and said not to use the arm. Pretty hard not to use it," and he gave the horse-stick an extra flourish.

"Yes, I suppose it was bursitis. It is very painful."

The road was narrow, but there were already plans for widening the Island roads. Now that cars were becoming more common, it was a bit awkward for two to meet. Today we were fortunate and thus far had not met any cars. Spruce trees were thick along each side, momentarily impeding our view of the red fields beyond.

"My Pa ain't too well. He has trouble with his back. A disk flies out of his back and he has to lie down and keep awful quiet 'til it goes back. That makes more work for me, and Mom ain't too well either. I have two brothers, but they went off to work in Hamilton. And tonight, I have to play the gitar at a dance after all me work at the farm is done." At the thought of this urgency, he pulled the reins, tapped at the horse and added a loud, "Gitup, there." Then we turned a corner and we were at Joe Morgan's gateway.

The Morgan home had been freshly white-washed, the green trimmings looked the same. There were no splashing ducks, but I saw a flock of geese in the adjoining field and some hens were pecking about the doorway.

Gina answered my knock at once. She was thin but looked quite well. She smiled happily. I looked at her closely for signs of unhappiness, after the smile of greeting had died away. There were none.

"How are you feeling, Gina?"

"Fine, now, I had a sore on my arm. It was the hardest thing to heal, but the doctor gave me a bottle of blue poison tablets to dissolve and soak dressings in that, and it worked great. It healed up."

"Was it bichloride of mercury?"

"Yes, that's it," She nodded her head.

Little Joseph was there hiding behind her dress, a pretty boy who came and stood beside me when Gina told him I had brought him. "Brought him," that surely meant that he had lived with me at some time in the past. At any rate, we must have been closely associated.

Lool came into the room. She looked quite tall in her blue and white checked dress. Although she had bobbed her hair and she was wearing high-heeled shoes, there always seemed to be something set or proper about Lool. I wondered if she were a bit like the prodigal's brother who stayed home while her sister went abroad behaving in a foolish fashion. But Gina wished Lool to have some praise and encouragement.

"Show her the mats you hooked, Lool," Gina said. "She has some beauties, and she took two prizes at the exhibition."

The mats were very nice and after we had admired them, Gina said, "Get your quilts, too, Lool. She made a beauty, a Dresden Plate, you know. All that work. She was offered twenty-five dollars for it."

We admired the quilt, then the conversation seemed to end. I looked at the wall in the little sitting room, and the motto "God Bless Our Home" was still there, as it had been that afternoon when I was frightened and upset.

"You have a new neighbour, a Mr. Richardson," I said.

"Yes," Gina did not know them, but had seen them in church. "Is she a bit queer? She was dressed funny for an elderly person in pale blue, well, a robin's-egg blue, really."

"I know her well," I said. "She is fond of pretty things and now that she has a chance to get them and wear them, she won't pass it up."

"I must call on them." Gina said as she rose to make tea. "There is a dance tonight in the hall in aid of something."

"You are going?"

"Yes," Gina said, but when I asked Lool about her going, she shook her head. "No, Dad is working late and somebody has to stay home." It seemed she was following in her role.

"I must show you my dress for the dance," Gina said. "I just got it from Eaton's." She slipped it down over her shoulders, her head and profile emerging from the top. She turned towards me and smiled. The material was of bright yellow rayon with a pleated bertha at the neck. The material, folded, looked not unlike feathers and the shining clips at the neckline like eyes – a bird of bright plumage.

"You will be quite grand, Gina. Do they all dress up at a country dance?"

"Oh no, some wear suits, some housedresses, some party dresses. They wear anything."

Joseph left my side and reached for an apple from a

large basket. He had had several, as there were cores and some half-eaten ones around the otherwise tidy room, each bearing a mark of small, pointed, milk teeth.

"They are yellow transparents. They won't hurt him," Gina said. "Would you care for one?"

"Not just now, thanks. I must be going."

At the door, Joseph waved bye-bye joyfully as if my going was a happy event.

"Goodbye for now... Goodbye," from Gina and Lool.

When I reached home, there was a letter from Martin. She was nursing in Charlottetown and had been out to the hospital and had talked with Fisher. There were some items of interest. One of our senior nurses had gone to Mt. Sinai Hospital in New York to take a postgraduate course, and the report from the hospital had been very favourable. The superintendent had written Miss Eden that she liked our nurse very much and would welcome more from her training school. Also, another graduate had gone to take up the duties of a matron in a hospital in Drumheller, Alberta. Soon we would hear that another bird has flown, I thought ruefully.

Saying it with Fish

Another afternoon, Uly had been sitting in the kitchen mending some harness when he looked up and said, "How about coming for a drive with me this evening? I have to see about getting help with the potatoes, and I will be passing Mrs. O'Brien's. You said you would like to see her. I could call for you on my way back."

This seemed to me to be a splendid idea.

"But Dad has taken the car to Hunter River, so we will have to take Old Bob. Do you mind?"

"No indeed." In fact, slow driving around the country in a carriage was of more interest than being rushed about in a car.

"How is Old Bob now?" I asked, thinking of my father's concern. He looked well as we hitched him to the wagon.

"He is all right, but he is old. We don't let him do much work. He is mostly out in the pasture. Dad would never sell him or let him go where he might be ill-treated," Uly said as we started on our journey.

We drove up past the pond where the road was shaded at one side by a wood of spruce, poplar and maple. One maple had turned bright red. A rabbit came out, saw us and froze, hoping it hadn't been observed. The iridescence of a river came to us through bordering trees.

We met a man in a wagon who seemed to be well known to Uly. He stopped to chat and dwelt on the weather and the fact that wheat hadn't been grown here in any great quantity because so much had been imported from the West. He relaxed completely, and putting one foot up on the dashboard of his carriage, he leaned back prepared to have a good discussion of various things. Uly introduced him as Mr. Jones. He had a fair, good-natured face, and he looked at me thoughtfully and with speculation. As if I were dreaming up business, he said doubtfully, "I don't think there is much sickness around the country just now. We did have a bad spell of the flu."

"Well, I am not thinking of a case now," I said. "I am hoping to have a rest, I have been busy."

Then Uly, thinking he had better get on, pulled on the reins, and we clattered along the dirt road until we came to Mrs. O'Brien's home. Her house was grey, unpainted, but with some red ornamental trimming. There were some shade trees and a bed of asters in the front, but no animals were in evidence, as Mrs. O'Brien was away from home much of the time. But she was home this evening and answered my knock at once.

I was pleased to see Mrs. O'Brien. We had been so

closely associated in the past. Many days and nights, we had watched in anxiety. We were thrown together so much that now we couldn't be indifferent to each other's welfare.

"Come in, Nurse, and I'll be after makin' us a cup of tea." Then she hurried to tell me of a case she had had. She was pleased with the social and financial status of her patient. She seemed to take it as an honour to herself that she could nurse in a home where – "They had a beautiful bathroom upstairs and a downstairs toilet too, and two cars. And a woman hired to cook their meals, too, and floors all polished, you could see your face in them and a radio – they didn't bother none with the old phonographs with them horns they had before. And they had a telephone upstairs and downstairs. You didn't have to run up and down – a good thing with my heart the way it is. And that woman had kidney trouble and gastritis of the liver – and she worked awful hard. She had a lovely garden and she took sixteen pills a day."

Here she paused for breath and I broke in with a statement regarding nursing in homes where the people cared a great deal about appearances. "Well, I nursed in a place where everything was very grand. You know, the maid wore a cap when she served the meals, and we ate by candlelight in the evening. The silver and china were of the finest, but the little girl of the house watched for her chance to kick me in the shins. There was no kindness in that place. I like to nurse where there is more down-to-earth sincerity and kindness."

"Yes, ain't it the truth!" Mrs. O'Brien said, as if this had been her idea. "Stuck-up places is no good."

"I am getting a bit tired of maternity cases," I said, "I don't like giving chloroform. If one gives too much, it is hard on the heart and if there isn't enough given, the patient suffers too much."

"Oh, I don't mind giving it. Just give it until the patient starts to snore."

I thought that might be too much, but I said nothing.

Then Mrs. O'Brien said, "I know a good medicine to take down a fever. A few drops of aconite does it great. They used to give it to horses. It was just by accident that I found out about it."

"But that might be very dangerous, Mrs. O'Brien. It said in our *Materia Medica* that 'the patient may have a tingling sensation and a few drops can kill.' I would be afraid to have anything to do with aconite. It is such a powerful poison."

"Well, I never had a bit of trouble with it," she said. She hurried on to tell about Annie Maude Barnes. "You never seen the likes of the change in her. She got new teeth for herself and got her hair frizzed and got gold rimmed glasses. And John is up and around, but he still takes a lot of medicine. Some men said when they saw a man driving down the road with a cart, 'That's John Barnes going for his winter supply of medicine. Ain't it awful to take so many pills and the like?'"

While she was preparing lunch, I looked up at the pictures which Mrs. O'Brien had chosen to decorate her walls. "That's a picture of Patrick taken when he was going to the war. I had it enlarged and coloured and framed. I am sorry I went to that expense when things turned out the way they did," Mrs. O'Brien said as she put a tray, laden with cups and saucers, on the table.

If the picture had been coloured correctly, Patrick O'Brien had been a fair man with reddish hair. The frame of the picture seemed to come too near and close in on him, and I thought perhaps that was the way he had felt life to be, cramped and closed in.

"How many years does it have to be before a man is declared dead?" asked Mrs. O'Brien as she came with a plate of cake and cookies. "Patrick has been gone six years now, and I want to declare him dead. Do you know, a nice gentleman and I became acquainted. I nursed his wife before she died. We worked so hard over her, and he was so good and knowledgeable, I liked him. Well, he asked me if it would be all right if he came to see me some evenin'. I can't see why it wouldn't be all right so he came last week, and brought me a whole case of canned lobster. He lives out near the shore, and he may come again any evening now."

"Here? Were you expecting him tonight?" I asked. I noticed that Mrs. O'Brien was rather dressed up. She was wearing a rose dress of some figured material, and she had added colour to her cheeks. She was not unattractive. I tried to see her as the nice gentleman might see her.

"His name is John Henry Walker and he has a lovely home with all his wife's sofa pillows and mats and quilts that she made, and he has two barns and a hen-house and a little house for the dog in the front yard."

There was a pause here as Mrs. O'Brien ate, and I broke the silence by saying that I had gone to Montreal and done some Public Health work there.

"Glory be to God, Nurse, why would you go clear away to Montreal? All alone amongst all them foreigners? Your father must not have been happy about it. I heard of awful doings in them big cities. Patrick used to tell me."

"In Montreal they have courses in Public Health Nursing and also Practical Nursing," I said. I saw at once this was an unfortunate remark. Mrs. O'Brien probably thought I was suggesting that she take the course. She seemed angry and perhaps with reason. One does not tell a professor that he should study more. Her face went white for a minute, with only the rouge standing out, then there was a line of demarcation around her ears where the white met a deep red. I did not know how I could soothe her. I ate her cake, which was very good, and looked out of the window to see a car drive in the yard.

"The saints be praised. Yes, it's him, Mr. Walker." Mrs. O'Brien hurried to the door.

Mr. Walker came in. He was a tall, well-built man, very much tanned from the sun. He had a very serious expression, and considering what Mrs. O'Brien had told me, life had dealt seriously with him. He had come bearing gifts. He put a large box of chocolates, a bundle of dried codfish carelessly wrapped, and a beautiful bouquet of flowers on the table. The gifts showed his regard for Mrs. O'Brien, but I had never heard of "saying it with fish." However,

Mrs. O'Brien was practical, and I knew she would be pleased.

I wanted to leave now if only Uly would come back to call for me. This was a time when I felt I was an unnecessary third.

And then something happened so unbelievable that it seemed a misplaced page out of another life. The door opened and a tall, fair man came in. It was Patrick O'Brien. He came forward and would have embraced Mrs. O' Brien, but she had turned pale and sank into a chair as if she might faint.

"I thought you were dead, Patrick," she said when she had recovered enough to sit up and look with great interest at her husband who now stood before her shabbily dressed and very thin, but smiling.

Now Mr. Walker, who must have felt very much out of place, came forward and said that he would be going along now.

"You see," he said awkwardly, "Your wife nursed my wife before she died, and she was so kind and good I wanted to bring her a little present."

Patrick O'Brien looked over at the presents on the table, and perhaps because he was Irish, he laughed. "Sure, it's all right," he said to Mr. Walker who left at once, taking with him all Mrs. O'Brien's thoughts of the pretty home and the two barns and hen-house.

"Why didn't you write, Patrick?"

"I was always waiting, thinking ways might take a good turn and I could send home some money, but instead of getting better, they got worse. The poverty in the West is terrible. Men left their homes and had to beg for bread. I have been riding on the freight cars, going from place to place to get work. I didn't have to beg, but I was often hungry. I would have been glad of some of your cooking, many a time."

When Patrick spoke of being hungry, Mrs. O'Brien softened somewhat. She liked everyone to be well fed including herself.

"You didn't know we had a baby."

"Where is it?"

"Out in the churchyard. She was a lovely, little girl, and I took her to the hospital, but she had a quick kind of T.B. and they couldn't save her. I got a lovely little tombstone for her." And then looking at her husband closely she said, "And you never got that birthmark off yet, Patrick."

"To hell with the birthmark! Are you crazy or somethin'? Your child died and your husband almost starved to death and you begin fussin' about a birthmark. How about getting me a bite to eat?" His expression softened and he began to laugh.

As Mrs. O'Brien started to prepare a meal for her hungry husband, she seemed to return easily to her former role of housewife.

Mr. O'Brien then produced some beer to celebrate his homecoming. They invited me to stay and have a glass with them, but Uly had just come for me, so I left, happy to make my escape from the scene of so many conflicting emotions.

When I told Uly about Mr. O'Brien's return, he was surprised, then said, "He can get plenty of work here on the Island, now that potato-digging is beginning, and there is work on the roads, too. They are paving all the principal highways, which is a good thing."

I wondered if Mrs. O'Brien would continue nursing now that her husband had returned. She hadn't mentioned plasters or goose grease. People were depending more on prescriptions as they had come on the market, and more and more, the home remedies seemed a thing of the past.

We drove on. The soft night air was scented with the odour of spruce and pine. Then from the distance, in the direction of the river, came a long, drawn-out plaintive cry. "I think that is a loon," Uly said. "We seldom hear them here."

Abegweit! This Is My Home

And so I continued. Sometimes my cases were easy, sometimes hard. Sometimes acquaintances developed into friendships lasting through the years. Many cases involved long hours of nursing, but whenever possible, I would return home to the quiet of the countryside.

I was at home enjoying a sunny autumn day when I was called to Charlottetown to relieve a tired nurse for one night.

The case was down on Water Street near the C.N. railway depot, where the patient had a suite in a rather old-style hotel. He was having severe asthmatic attacks that were relieved by adrenalin given hypodermically. He was not confined to his bed but could not be left alone because the attacks were severe and would come without warning.

I arrived a few minutes before eight. The lobby reeked of cigar smoke, and a couple of elderly men sat in large leather armchairs with spittoons conveniently beside them.

The lady at the desk said that my patient, Mr. Boyce, was indeed there. She continued, "He is at the top – Room 401. Take the elevator."

When I reached the top floor, the nurse was waiting in the corridor, already dressed in street clothing and wearing large, hooped earrings. Her white teeth showed prominently as she smiled and greeted me. "I'm very glad you could come, as I was up much of last night," she said, looking at me intently. "Mr. Boyce had a bad attack and needed a hypo. He did not sleep at all well so will probably sleep tonight. But come in now and meet him."

The patient had been lying down in his bed but rose slowly to a sitting posture as we entered. He was a middle-aged man of considerable bulk, dressed in an expensive-looking black satin dressing gown with brocade lapels, and he was wearing yellow pajamas of some silky material. A copy of the Montreal Star was on his bed.

After the introductions, Miss Begg, whom I was replacing, went to the dressing table. She said, "If you will come here a minute, Nurse, I'll explain about the medicine. If he has an attack, the hypo needle may be boiled on this little electric stove, and you will find food and drink in the refrigerator in the corridor. Now, do you think there is anything else before I go?"

"No, I can't think of anything else," I said thoughtfully as I went into the corridor with her. "I hope he has a good night and that you will get some rest, too."

While waiting for the elevator, she whispered, "I think you will be all right. He seemed to be quite taken with you. By the way, you can get some rest on the settee in the other room when he settles down."

In the bedroom, Mr. Boyce looked me over carefully with piercing dark eyes. The air was heavy with incense. I now saw the source – in the corner of the room was a small Buddha with a joss stick burning in front of it. I wondered if the heavy air might be disturbing or irritating to anyone with asthma.

"Doesn't the incense affect your asthma?" I asked.

"Oh no, Miss MacRae. I have lived in the Orient and I am very used to it." Then he explained that he had moved from Montreal to a summer hotel at Dalvay and had come to the city for treatment when the attacks came on him. He had found this hotel near the hospital, and here he would have to remain until he could take the long sea voyage back to Shanghai where he had an export-import business. After this exchange, Mr. Boyce said, "I'd like a back rub," as if expecting instant and automatic service. He seemed to be used to having much attention, I judged from the matter-of-fact way in which he spoke. I could easily imagine him clapping his hands and servants materializing out of the shadows to do his bidding. But here was only a nurse. Whether he needed the back rub or not, I couldn't very well refuse his request, and I was soon at the old familiar task.

That done, he looked up at me and queried, "You are not staying here in Charlottetown after tonight? Why not? Do you have a boyfriend?"

"No, I am leaving tomorrow to go back home to the

country," I said, hoping that would answer both questions. "What about boyfriends?" he persisted.

"Well, yes," I said hesitantly. This seemed the best answer now, as I felt intuitively that he was about to offer himself in that capacity.

"You tell me where you live on Prince Edward Island, and I will come and see you before I leave, when I am better," he said.

"All right," I said warily, "But now I feel very tired. Would you mind if I went to my room now since you are feeling comfortable?"

"Yes, Yes, Nurse, go along," he said sulkily. As I got up to go, he unexpectedly caught my hand and raised it to his lips.

I snatched my hand away. "Goodnight," I said firmly, and went quickly to the other room of the suite. But I couldn't lock my door because I was still on duty, and I was very conscious of the fact that the only way out of the suite was through the bedroom of Mr. Boyce!

I threw myself wearily on the settee, fully dressed in my uniform, and pulled the blanket over me that had been put there for the other nurse. I was too uneasy to sleep, but I could rest a bit. From the open door, I could see the image of the Buddha. He was supposed to personify peace. I stared at the head slightly bowed in contemplation. Then I heard my patient's regular breathing and thought with relief that he was asleep.

A noise woke me and my heart thumped. I had fallen asleep after all, but it seemed like a very short time. Now was my patient asleep? Then I heard him get out of bed and walk out to the corridor. He would be just going to the bathroom. Soon I heard him return and settle himself in his bed. Then… "Miss MacRae, can you come here? I can't sleep."

I pretended not to hear the call, and then my fear and uneasiness changed to terror, because Mr. Boyce had again left his bed, and I could tell by the shuffling footsteps that he was coming into my room. I got up, put on the light, and faced my patient who stood there with sulky determination.

"I want you to come and talk to me," he said, "I can't sleep."

Now that I faced him, some of my courage returned. I was angry, too. "You have no right to come in here, and you know it," I spat the words out with all the force I was capable of. "I came as a nurse, to help you, that is all."

"But I am paying you good money," he said plaintively, and continued to move towards me.

"Go back to bed at once. I am going to leave you if you don't behave," I hissed. As he reached for my arm and tried to pull me down on the settee, he stumbled and I heard him gasp. He was struggling for breath. "I'm smothering," he choked out. "Get the medicine, quick, Nurse!"

This was the only time in my nursing duty that I was glad to have a patient suffer an attack of any kind! I prepared the hypo, gave it quickly, and watched him relax and very soon fall asleep. He should sleep until morning, I thought. And morning will come, I assured myself.

At eight o'clock, Miss Begg appeared, happily rested,

and asked how the night had been. I said only that Mr. Boyce had had an attack and I had given the adrenalin. I had written on the chart. "Attack at 2:30 a.m. Hypo given, then slept." He was still sleeping when I left the hotel. I decided that in the future I would find out more about surroundings and conditions before taking a case.

The morning air was refreshing as I walked out of the hotel and caught the sea breeze. Some men were loading potatoes into a schooner at the dock. Their voices echoed in the early morning still air. On the street, small replicas of the sun danced on the moving trucks. Stores with names like Karachi, Amed, Bercovice, and a laundry shop of Lee Wong's over-shadowed Mrs. Dunn's tiny dress shop where some dainty hand-made blouses and sweaters were on display. The East had come to the West.

I wandered up a side street and came to the cathedral, large and imposing, of dark square-cut stone, towering over the surrounding buildings. A woman came out of the main entrance, and I glanced at her curiously as I met her. Her face had an expression of peace and happiness. I walked up the steps and entered the church. Here in the dim, cloistered stillness, I tried to think why the certitude of youth had given way to incertitude. Perhaps the jarring realities of life had shaken a youthful faith, but standing here, I knew only that the woman had found comfort. Here, she had found something not of the earth. Others were coming in to pray, their heads covered, their genu-flections graceful, their faces serious as they knelt to pray.

After a while, I stole out, not wanting to break the

silence, and went back down to the wharf. My good spirits returned and I felt that I couldn't be sad on this bright morning.

Perhaps now was the time to make a complete change in my life. I could go back to Montreal or to Toronto, which would mean that I would be close enough to my aging father and aunt to see them occasionally, and yet enjoy the comforts and opportunities of the big city. I could go on a cruise, or travel to California! But as pictures of glamorous cities and exotic places flashed through my mind, there also came a picture of Bill Martin. In a twilight walk by the river on the Labour Day weekend, he had spoken of marriage, but I had been called away, and there had been no time to consider the question. I knew there would never be a dull moment for me in Bill's home, and my thoughts kept straying back to Bedeque and the welcome that I felt sure awaited me there. It was possible that the unpleasant experience of the previous night might have been the catalyst I needed to open another door, to accept the challenge that I had evaded thus far.

At the wharf, the potato boat was still being loaded. As the men slung the bags of potatoes from the trucks with an unvarying rhythm, I watched them, mesmerized. Yes, these are my people and this is my home. The water gently lapped on the wooden pier. The lapping was like rocking, the rocking of a cradle. "Abegweit, cradled on the waves," had been the Micmac name for the Island. Now I knew that I would stay here, and that my destiny would be on Prince Edward Island, whatever the outcome would be.

Afterword

The central characters in *Try the Goose Grease* are based on the author's family and close friends, and although the descriptions of patients are fictitious, the medical cases were true.

Helen and Bill Martin are characters inspired by her friend Jane Tuplin, also a nurse, and Jane's brother, Fred Tuplin, whom Dolly went on to marry. They lived at Tuplin's Mill, a lovely spot in Indian River, where a water wheel ran a flour and sawmill and which became an inspiration for many of her paintings.

About the Author

MARY ISABEL (DOLLY) MACDONALD TUPLIN was born in 1894 in New Glasgow, PEI. She graduated from Prince Edward Island Hospital in 1917 and nursed in Massachusetts, Los Angeles and Montreal as well as on Prince Edward Island. But she wove her novel around the people who captured her heart in the rural areas of PEI.

Skilled at portraying scenes with both paintbrush and pen, Dolly brought her characters and Island landscapes to life. She captured the spirit of PEI in her watercolour and oil paintings, one of which is reproduced for the cover of this edition.

Dolly died in 1975, at the age of eighty-one and was

laid to rest at the United Church cemetery in Margate, PEI.

The first and second editions of *Try the Goose Grease* were published posthumously in 1988 and 1990, respectively, and were followed by a play of the same name which was adapted for the stage by Alice Anna Reese and entered into the New Voices playwriting competition in 1999.

— L. Kormos, J. Nunes, F. Nunes (current edition),
and P. Stanyer (first and second editions), Editors.